A Follow Your Heart Novel

Linda Phillips

A special thanks to Melange Books and Kimberly for the much needed help in making this story sparkle, just like Talia sparkles in the story.

Chapter One

Follow your heart, even if love takes you to the stars in the heavens or
down into
the depths of the sea. Reach high...

As she sits in despair and questions why,
She feels the brush of an angel's wing as it passes by,
A smile and comforted heart, no longer the need to cry.

~

The day was dark, even eerie. The sun's rays begged to break through and indulge mankind with its cheerfulness, but ominous clouds filtered them out. Still, something was odd: a sparkly glow beamed a path through the forest to a tower of a shabby, unloved cottage. The glistening presence was unexplainable.

Droopy eyes stared out a window. A bewildered beauty rested her head on her hands.

All day.

Every day.

That same heavenly glow that filled the pathway through the forest reflected off her skin as if heaven itself was showcasing her beauty. Was she an angel? Or maybe the good Lord above wanted the world to notice her. But why? What made her so different from everyone else?

Twirling and humming a song in front of the window, a pulchritudinous young lady, filled to the brim with inner beauty, donned a cheerful front. With a forced smile, she pranced, and her long, blonde, almost-white hair glittered as it fluttered and settled on the middle of her thigh.

Wherever she abided, glistening dew sparkled—whether around the exterior of her room or the trails where she walked. The tower where she had been held prisoner for five years had strong iron bars covering the windows, and the door was bolted shut with a heavy block of wood across the outside of it.

"Hello up there, Lord. You're my best friend in the whole world. The only friend in the whole world."

Glittery tears trailed her face, and she tried to catch her breath from gut-wrenching sobs. Gathering her composure, she leaned on the window and sang a sweet song. The soft, alluring melody lured the forest animals near, like a fairy tale coming to life. She saw reflections of their eyes peeking out of the forest, and her eyes followed them, roving up high to the sky and down low to the ground. Her innocent, tear-stained face beamed a smile, and new, fresh tears formed. She loved the creatures of the forest, and they loved her.

Feeling a sensation on her arm, she rubbed the spot, wondering if a feather from an angel's wing brushed against her. Her arms and neck prickled with goosebumps. Her eyes searched. She dragged her fingers softly across her skin, trying to imitate the feel of a feather. The sensation, imagined or not, deserved a glimpse to the heavens, producing a grateful smile across her face.

"You have not abandoned me. Thank you for reminding me,

my Lord," she spoke in a hushed tone. "And as You instructed Your children, I pray in sincerity for the salvation of my captors, although, in truthfulness, I despise them as much as they despise me. But they deserve to know Your love just as much as I do. Please enlighten their path, dear Lord."

Talia sat back down on the bed, her Bible in hand. She turned to Psalms 6, reading verses 6-10. "I am weary with my sighing; every night I make my bed swim, I dissolve my couch with my tears. For the Lord has heard the voice of my weeping..."

How is it even possible to produce tears after years of sobbing?

Her hand rubbed the tattered and stained sheets softly, feeling the dampness of her tears where she had swum in them the previous night. She sighed and glanced at the wooden crates, her abductors' idea of a couch still stained with a trail of her tears from last night. As she went to the window, a thought popped into her mind. Looking upwards, she meekly prayed: "You have heard my weeping. I just know it, Lord. I feel it in my soul. I can't wait to meet your servant, David. We certainly have a lot in common. Have a pleasant day, my Lord. I await eagerly for my rescue."

Was she imagining it, or did the forest animals have tears in their eyes? With tender eyes, she blew them a kiss.

Talia loved the small village of Bibury, which sat among the hilly Cotswold region and was often called England's most beautiful town, with a population of around 627. The River Coln ran through the main street, while lush meadows surrounded olden stone cottages with charming two-sided roofs. But that's where her abduction occurred—in Bibury, England, part of the civil parish in Gloucestershire. The reason for her capture was simple: greed—a plot to blackmail her parents.

She leaned her ear against the bolted door to hear the conversation in the living room.

"Let's hang on to the wench for a while longer," the leader

remarked. "Just look at her. She is worth far more than her parents could give. Perhaps we could sell Talia to a rich king or prince once she gets older. I know someone who can direct me to the right person. When they see her unexplainable beauty, we'll have many offers. I mean, who wouldn't want her for a wife or mistress or just to look at? If she looks this enchanting as a child, just imagine what she will look like as she grows older."

Her body trembled as she listened. She ran to the mattress on the floor, a sad imposter for a bed, jumping under the torn-up blankets. Sparkly tears trickled down her cheeks.

"Why do they hate me so? I have followed their orders. I speak nicely to them, even though they are grotesque," she said with a shaky whisper. She hiccupped and licked the fallen tears that flowed over her lips. Holding her hands together underneath her chin, she quaked, praying that God would have mercy on her.

Talia's parents, Lord Oliver and Freya Brennyinn, searched year after year for their beloved daughter. Eventually, the village concluded that she had drowned. Her boat was found floating on the river, and inside, wildflowers dotted the boat floor next to a mysterious dab of a sparkling, watery substance that couldn't be identified. They dragged the river for miles, but Talia's body was never found.

In the evenings, Freya aimlessly wandered the estate. One night, she discovered their housekeeper, Adelaide, sitting at the kitchen table crying with Twiggly, the butler. At that moment, Freya understood her daughter's impact on all who knew her.

The small community mourned their beloved loss. Talia had earned their love with a caring, adventurous, and fun disposition.

The day Talia was abducted, Lord had Brennyinn offered a

reward of a million dollars to anyone who could identify her whereabouts. It was everything he had in the world—and, unfortunately, what he didn't have. Should she be found, he would have to borrow money. His family knew nothing about the financial situation he hid from them.

Still, financial ruin would be worth it if only he could have his daughter back. Like the other household members, Lord Brennyinn also fell apart in despair. His body weight wasted away from being unable to eat, and his sobs echoed throughout the house at night. His clothes hung limply on his frail body, and many days, the house staff and Freya would watch Lord Brennyinn push himself up out of a chair, bracing his feet against the front legs to keep him from falling.

After nearly five years of imprisonment, Talia's abductors still hadn't sold her to men of wealth and stature—the men wanted to wait until she had grown into a teenager. Plus, many of the potential buyers believed her appearance was manipulated. Talia overheard her abductors say, "If I hear one more person ask how she could possibly sparkle like that, we may need to discuss just cutting our losses and disposing of her."

Talia held a fairy-tale book in her hands. Reading stories of a knight in shining armor caused her to stare out the window and daydream about the day her knight would rescue her. She turned the book over and returned to the windowsill, resting her chin on her hands with a sigh of defeat. It was a silly thing to imagine. What else was there to dream about, though? Loneliness? The lustful eyes of her captors? Each day was the same, day after dreary day.

As she stared blankly at the wall, anger replaced her tears, and she bit down on her lip, drawing blood. *What would happen if I tried to escape?* she wondered, staring blankly at the ceiling. She jumped off the bed and paced, her forehead wrinkled. *What could be worse: being a prisoner the rest of my life or perhaps dying and spending a glorious life in heaven with my Lord and Savior?* She smiled at the thought. She knew one of the men would bring in a food tray later, so she planned her move.

That evening, her jailer, Norman, brought her some food—that's what they called it, anyway. As he turned to set the tray on the wooden crate, Talia jumped off the bed and ran out the open door. She made it to the cottage's front door, and she had her hand on the doorknob when Percy, one of her abductors, opened the door from the outside. She sucked in a fearful breath as he grabbed her. She clenched her eyes shut and bit the bottom of her lip, struggling to be free of his clenching, painful grip.

It happened so fast. He pulled her up in his arms and squeezed her so tight she couldn't breathe. Her face turned gray. Then, he threw her down, and she hit the floor with a thud while another accomplice, Harry, closed the front door. Percy pressed his foot down on her stomach, and she gasped for air again. For a glorious second, he removed his foot, but then, he yanked her to her feet and slapped her face.

"Oof," she murmured through the seething pain. Her hands covered her face, and she cowered, falling to the floor and curling into a ball. "Stop, please stop," she cried.

Once again, Percy yanked her up by her hair until their faces were uncomfortably close. He glared into her fearful eyes. She trembled.

"Next time, I'll kill you. Now, move. Back to your room." He shoved her toward the room, and she walked in slowly, wincing with each small step. The door slammed closed so loudly, it caused her to jump. As she heard the piece of wood bolt the door, she lowered herself slowly on the mattress and whimpered softly.

Forcing herself to quit crying, she listened. They were laughing. *Why do they hate me so? Why not just kill me and get it over with?*

Why? But she knew why. She had heard their scheming, so she knew how rich she would make them.

She rocked back and forth slowly, squinting her eyes in pain with each movement. She tried to look heavenward, but it was too painful. *Why Lord? Why?*

Overwhelmed with pain, she collapsed back on the mattress and fell into a fitful dream of the past.

～

Sitting on her windowsill, she stared out at the river and saw a heavenly glow. On impulse, she climbed out and jumped into the boat, even though her parents would never allow her to go out in the evening.

"Lord above, your creation is magnificent," she said.

The heavens brightened a path that was too intriguing to ignore, and as if God was guiding the boat, it floated to a location she couldn't resist exploring.

She hopped out of the boat, trampling through a ground cover of bramble and ivy, stumbling onto the most ineffable spot in the whole world. A modest waterfall flowed into a small pool before escaping into the River Coln. She followed a rock path along the pool into a secret underground pond filled with a thick, glittering liquid. The sweet odor was unlike anything she had ever smelled. I'll call it "Dew of Heaven," she said, her voice echoing in the cave. Using her hand as a makeshift cup, she sipped the mysterious water, which tasted sweet like nectar.

In her dream, she saw a flash, and "Dew of Heaven" melded into another scene. She was taking a boat ride, stroking the paddles down the River Coln, when she spotted some burly men passing by in a boat. They smiled at her, and a pang of fear and consternation rippled through her body. She locked eyes with one of the men as they floated past her. He smiled a gap-toothed grin with one of his front teeth missing. Talia noticed his torn, stained clothing, and the pong of the men's putrid body odor lingered as they passed.

The dream severed, Talia's eyes flew open, and her mouth formed an 'O' in a silent scream. *Lord, please give me pleasant dreams. I don't want to relive that day ever again.*

Chapter Two

Marquess Chatwin Kendrick Alexander Riley George arrived back at Bibury on a mission of God—or so he convinced himself, even though God, technically, had nothing to do with his decision. Truthfully, it was because of God that his life had been ruined; someone must pay dearly for that.

He decided to grab something to eat and listen to the town gossip, so he disguised himself with an extra-large hoodie, a worn pair of jeans, and dark sunglasses so that no one would recognize him.

Would you look at that, the Café at Coln is still in business? It always had good food.

"Would you like a cuppa, sir?" the genuinely friendly, middle-aged waitress asked.

"I would, please."

"I'll be right back with it." She set the tea down on the table. "Now, what can I get for ye?"

He studied the menu and noticed they returned a brekkie old-time favorite for the day. With delight in his voice, he answered, "French toast and grilled pears, please."

"Excellent choice, sir."

Chatwin scanned the charming, cobblestone café. He couldn't dismiss the glorious scents floating around the café, teasing his stomach. He held his hand over his stomach, hoping no one could hear the bear growling inside. The folks were smiling and jabbering. Surprisingly enough, no one was staring at their cell phone.

Chatwin was envisioning a world without mobiles when a customer suddenly lifted a cell phone to his ear. "Darn. You had to go and ruin it, mister," Chatwin whispered. "Humans are idiots."

Despite his disguise, a few of the young women in the café stared at him. He gave them a sneering look that caused them to turn their blushing faces away. "Trust me, ladies, you don't want to mess with me," he said to himself.

"Here you are, sir. Syrups are right here on the table."

"It smells and looks heavenly," he replied.

The waitress was friendly and not coquettish in the least. He appreciated that. "Are you passing by or visiting?" she asked.

He had to be careful how he worded his response. He had planned this personal mission for years. Pretending to be a photographer, he replied, "I am visiting. However, I will spend most of my time in the forest regions looking for the best and most natural scenic views to photograph. Any suggestions on which direction to take?"

"That be a tough one. Every way you go has breathtaking views. I would rent a boat, take a trip down the River Coln, and get out into the forest. Paddle, then stop, and keep doing that. There is untouched beauty in all directions."

"Thank you. I'll consider it. Oh, miss, is the Viscount still living in your lovely area?"

She turned around and walked back toward him. "Yes, that be Lord Brennyinn. A good chap, he is."

"Does he live around here?"

"Aye, just above the hills over there." She pointed in the direction.

"Has he been at Bibury long, and does he have a family?" He already knew the answer, but he wanted to hear an honest description from a resident of the area.

The server replied enthusiastically, enjoying an opportunity to share a little gossip. "Aye, he has held that position for quite a lengthy time. After our first glorious duke and his wife passed away, their son disappeared and hasn't been heard from since. Terrible, terrible circumstances."

"I see," he replied. "That *does* sound terrible."

"Aye, but that not be the worst. When the son disappeared, so did the jobs, and now, many folks are suffering and contemplating moving away for work. This place has been near and dear to these fine folks, and the thought of having to move is sad and sure to turn this beloved village into a ruin. We feel it has been cursed."

"A curse, you say? Do you really believe that?"

"Aye," she replied. "And only the Marquess can save us. Our parish councilors are beloved by the folks in the village, but the epidemic has torn down our economy, and we are certain the marquess could get us back on our toes. If only he would come back to us."

"What about Lord Brennyinn? Does he not help?"

"Well, he, himself, is quite distraught. About five years ago, Lord Brennyinn's daughter went missing. They finally declared her dead and held the funeral a few days ago. She was an angel of God, for certain."

So, they've declared her dead, he thought. "Do you think the Marquess' disappearance is related to the girls' disappearance?" he asked to keep the waitress talking.

"Possibly. They were close, the two of them. At first, the princess and Marquess Chatwin were inseparable. They played and frolicked in the forest. Both were kindhearted, helping those in need. But as they grew older, the marquess was being prepped and pruned for his role, so they spent less time together. I could see the sadness in Miss Talia's eyes. She understood the necessity of his time, but she missed him terribly. She went around the town helping anyone in need, anyone lonely, any injured animal. That girl was one of a kind, worthy to be a fairy-tale princess."

The waitress sat in a booth across from Chatwin to continue her story.

"One day at the park, she and Chatwin were playing. I was sitting on a bench and heard them playing *Beauty and the Beast*. She called him a beast, and he got mad and yelled back at her that he was *not* a beast. That went on for a few more minutes before they raced each other around the park. That comment, though, it stuck with me."

"Why did that comment stick with you?" he asked.

"Oh, sir, please heed caution. It may be just folklore, but there be stories of a mean ole beast who lives deep within the forest. The folks say he can take on the form of a man or beast at any given time. He has never harmed the hair nor bones of any of these folks, though, but he has a frightful temper and can turn in a bloody second."

"So you believe the beast took the missing child?"

"It's possible. It's just gossip, but people say that the beast is waiting for the right time to seek revenge for some downright dastardly deeds befallen on him."

"Interesting," he said.

The waitress stood and smiled at him. "Although, as big and strong as ye look, he may fear you." She chuckled at her witty remark.

"Aye, but that is tragic and concerning. I'll be careful, miss. No worries. I'm good to go. Thank you for the information."

Now, his plans would change. His teeth ground, and his jaw tightened. He wanted to smash the table in two, but he managed to hold it together long enough to finish breakfast.

As he stood to leave the café, he glanced up and saw Mr. Brown and Mr. Jones. *Mr. Jones will definitely recognize me. I need to get out of here, now. My, how they have aged. Poor Mr. Brown looks like he is in pain with each step.*

He was really fond of Mr. Brown as a child. His eyes teared up underneath his sunglasses.

Over the years, Chatwin had grown an awful, scruffy beard, and his hair almost touched his shoulders. His hood covered his head in public, no matter the time of the year. Occasionally, one of the townspeople would get a good look at him, but after a few moments, they would scream in horror, thinking they recognized him.

As he walked toward the door, he felt everyone staring at him. He knew he gave off a frightful vibe. On his way out of the café, his eyes wandered to an old, withered paper stuck on the bottom of the window. It was torn, and the shrubs had grown up and covered what was left of it. He lifted it and saw that it was a flier offering a reward of some sort, but the words were faded and torn too badly to read on.

However, he could make out a picture of a girl with long, golden-white hair. She looked to be a child of twelve to fourteen years old. His eyes stared in wonder. "How tragic," he mumbled under his breath.

He dropped the flier and walked away, focused on his mission. After picking up his gear, he hiked through the forest for hours, snapping pictures to make the disguise look legit, should anyone question him. Exhausted from the hiking, a deep sigh escaped his lips, accompanied by a yawn that lasted for seconds.

A pine marten ran past about ten feet away. He snapped a picture. When a red deer stag leaped across the meadow, he yawned again. He was exhausted after walking for six hours. *Time to set up my tent and fix myself a scrumptious canned beef stew dinner.*

After clearing a spot to make a safe fire, the spoon clinked against the pot as he stirred the stew with a blank stare. He glanced at the river about fifteen feet away, which would make it easy to gather water for dousing the fire when it was time to sleep. The rushing current of the river had a calming effect on him as it splashed against the rocks. A squirrel sat on the edge of a branch, nibbling on an acorn and watching him.

"Hello, little fellow—little gal—whatever the heck you are. Don't you just love the peacefulness out here?" Chatwin leaned back in the grass, resting on his elbows, chewing on a piece of grass. The squirrel sat still—only its mouth moving as it ate the acorn it held in its paws. Crack-crack-crack.

Chatwin laid his head back and closed his eyes, listening. "The symphony of chirping and stridulating is relaxing. Most people claim it to be annoying. Do you?" he asked the squirrel. Then, he shook his head and smiled. "Not very talkative, are you? Oh well, I'll talk, and you can listen. I have been so out of touch that I never kept up with the news around town. If I had, I wouldn't have made this trip for nothing."

The squirrel jumped to a higher branch when he elevated his voice.

"Subconsciously, my thoughts were urging me to keep looking, but now, they've declared her dead. Then again, they could be wrong. I read an article in an American newspaper about a young lady with fairy-tale beauty, discovered by a hiker. He said she was being held prisoner in a cabin on the outskirts of Bibury. The hiker managed to get close to the window and speak to her. Wanting to have something to remember her by, he snapped a picture. As the hiker ran away, he was spotted by one of the abductors. The hiker managed to escape and brought the authorities back to the cabin, but the abductors had moved her to another location."

Chatwin looked up at the squirrel perched on a branch in a tree.

"I think I'll keep hiking instead of calling it a night, and maybe, just maybe, I'll find her."

The squirrel grew bored with his chattering and moved to another branch.

"Well, excuse me for confiding in you, you flea and mite fur ball."

Suddenly, Chatwin put his head in his hands, squinted his eyes tightly, and bawled like a baby. The torn picture at the café hit him like a ton of bricks, and flashbacks plowed through his thoughts with a vengeance. He thought of the picture again. Even though she was innocent in all of this, justice needed to be upheld—if not by God, then by him.

Living like a hermit, with infrequent conversations between himself and the small crew of his estate, he was lonely, but that was how he wanted it—the way he demanded it. His few faithful assistants conducted all his business dealings electronically.

The day was at the twilight hour. He watched the sun disappear over the horizon. *What a beautiful sight.* He lay there as the sky turned silky black, interspersed with sparkling, blinking gemstones. Suddenly, he pushed his body up to get a better view of a bright, heavenly light, creating a pathway through the forest.

"I'll be back, little friend. I think I'll follow that pathway. It feels like it is calling—no begging me to follow it. I mean, just look at it. That's what any sensible person would have to conclude."

Chapter Three

Following the path, Chatwin heard voices off in the distance. With each step, the murmurs became clearer, and eventually, he could make out some of the words—expletives and something about a prince in a far-off country. His feet crunching leaves and sticks made it too difficult to hear, so he paused and bent down behind a huge tree to listen further.

"What do they mean, captive princess?" he whispered.

When the voices got closer, he considered returning to his camp to hide his belongings, but he spotted the men taking an alternate path, so he was confident they wouldn't notice his tent.

"I have to continue," he said to himself. "There must be a logical explanation for why this path is glistening."

As he continued, the lighted path grew brighter, and he felt his stomach perform a somersault with anxiety. When he bent down to examine the glowing path, his eyes locked onto the light, and he felt as if it had hypnotized him. Instinctively, his fingers touched the sparkling dew. He rubbed it between his fingers. It felt silky.

What is this substance? he wondered. He forced his eyes away from the ethereal liquid and spoke aloud. "Maybe I'm going mad from my lack of socialization because I *must* be losing my mind."

Chatwin continued walking, following the trail for thirty minutes, when he heard a faint sound like singing in the distance. Because the sun had sent, it was dark, but the odd glow made it easy for him to follow the path. The further he continued, the sound grew louder, and the singing voice was sweet and glorious.

There! He spotted a house. In the window, he saw a twirling whirl of glittery sparkles. "I have to get closer and see what is in that window," he whispered.

He crept slowly, looking side to side.

Then he saw her.

Paralyzed, he froze, staring at a young woman so beautiful, he couldn't believe his eyes.

"Why does she sparkle? It's like someone lit a sparkler at Guy Fawkes Night in the UK. Even her eyes are glowing. She can't be real." He slapped the side of his head to correct his vision. "This has to be a dream." He closed his eyes and opened them again. *Still there.* "Go up closer to the window, you dope," he said.

As he approached, he saw that heavy iron bars enclosed the window. Suddenly, he heard a crackling of debris, and he halted abruptly. A gigantic man emerged from around the house and stood in front of the window, holding a rifle.

"Who do those jerks think they are making me stay behind and guard her while they go to the local and meet some of their eager slappers? My mouth is watering for a lager. If I have to stay here one more day, I will take your measly womanhood from you, princess. You stand there looking like some goddess and expect me to suffer, ye wench? Nooo. You can't touch her—

she has to remain pure to be sold to a king or prince," he said mockingly, shaking his head from side to side.

He rested the gun at his side and ran his hand through his hair in frustration.

"Everyone else is enjoying some good ole evenin' delight. I'm a big fan of evenin' delight, myself. That princess may be skinny, but other than that, her perfectly shaped body is just begging to be touched," the man growled slowly, moving his head back and forth with lustful eyes. He swallowed hard. "If she tells anyone, I'll just kill 'er and say she got away when I brought supper to 'er."

Chatwin heard the door slam.

∾

Chatwin had to see her up close. Could she, perhaps, really be a princess? That's what the awful man called her.

He crept to the window and saw the heavenly light illuminating a bright glow around her. Staring in disbelief at her striking beauty, he noted her enticing but terribly thin-formed body. *She looks familiar. It's her,* he thought. *The girl from that old, torn picture on the window at the café. It's her. I'd bet my life on it.*

The swishing of branches and a heavy crackling of debris cautioned him to step back and hide behind a tree as someone walked toward him. Those familiar, rumbustious voices from thirty minutes ago were heading in Chatwin's direction.

∾

"You blithering idiot! How could ye forget our tickets?"

"I don't know. I was rushed."

"Now we're behind schedule, and we'll have to make up the time. I wanted to stop at the pub fer a while. Now we can't, and let's just hope you don't pay for tha.'"

"What does that mean?"

"Tha' means I don't need you with me on this trip. Tha' means if I lose me temper from a lack of satisfaction, this rock of a fist may make you pay." He shook his fist back and forth.

"I thought we were friends."

"Friends like you, who needs enemies? Now, shut up!"

Harry's thoughts immediately turned to lust. He could not look at her without wanting to rip her clothes off and extinguish his built-up desires. Maybe it was just the fact that she was off-limits that made him want her so.

"Wait, Harry," the other man said. "Look. It's Norman."

They looked through the window and saw their partner enter Talia's room with a plate holding a Bakewell tart and some chocolate candies.

"Thank you, Norman. What is the occasion?"

"Just wanted to give you something you like."

He looked at her with narrowed eyes and bared teeth. Then he closed the door as he licked his lips. Her face lit up with fright.

He unbuttoned his pants and said, "Now, I want ye to give *me* something *I* like. Let's just call it evenin' delight."

She darted away from him, screaming. "Please don't do this, Norman. Please."

He laughed with a coldness. "You'll enjoy it. I promise."

"No! Don't you dare touch me."

Chatwin heard screaming and felt helpless and uncertain of what to do. He couldn't call for help and jeopardize his new plan. Besides, there certainly wouldn't be any mobile service out here.

He would just have to fight all three of them, as he couldn't take the chance of them raping and killing her. *I knew I should have grabbed my handgun before setting out.*

As Chatwin stepped from the tree, the screaming stopped.

He ran to the window and peered inside. The girl was curled up on her bed, and the burliest of the three men was manhandling the girl's attacker, the one she called Norman. Norman's face was red as an apple. They disappeared from his view, and he heard the door slam shut. Then, he heard crashing furniture, fist blows, and someone crying in pain.

~

"What do you think ye were doing? Ye know she has to remain pure. I should kill you right now."

"We're brothers, Percy. You goin' to kill yer own brother?"

"If I have to, yeah."

"I have been in some bad situations with you," Norman said. "Stayed in some real dumps like this. Tha's all I mean to ye?"

"Yup! Right now, it does. Ya tried to deceive me and jeopardize a chance of us living the good life, not living in dumps like this. We're going to get a million dollars for 'er. Ye can't control yourself long enough to get that kind of money?"

"Yer right. I'm sorry, man, but sometimes I look at 'er, and I can feel just how good it would be to make 'er pay for knowing we're not allowed to touch her. She knows it. It won't happen again."

"That's right, because yer coming with me, and Harry will guard 'er. I'll kill you, Harry, if you mess up. Ye can't run or hide. Ye have no money, and I'll just kill you if ye do anything to jeopardize this exchange. The deal was tha' she has to be a virgin or no deal. Got it? Ye both knew tha."

"I don't want to stay here in this dump. Besides, she does things to my mind, and I can't think clearly. It wouldn't be a good idea to leave me alone with 'er," Harry replied.

"Well, I guess I should just kill ye now," Percy said.

"No! No! I'll keep it together. I promise."

Chapter Four

C hatwin moved away from the window. The scene of despair was heartbreaking, even though his intentions were in no way valiant. On the contrary, he was here to kidnap her himself.

She has to be Talia, with that white, blonde hair, but where did that sparkle come from? I can't feel sorry for her. It will ruin everything I planned all these years and finally have the guts to carry out.

Rubbing his forehead, he stared at the ground, arguing with himself. "*Have* I turned into a beast? Why can't I feel compassion for a young woman so mistreated and undeserving? I can't think about this right now. When the time is right, I'll break her out of there, but I won't let that beauty and charm nobble my chance at redemption. This is the only form of vengeance that will bring results."

He stood staring with a blank look on his face, remembering the circumstances that brought him here in the first place. Holding a grimaced expression, he looked around for a safe hiding place.

Grumbling to himself, he said, "I bet she doesn't even know about the crime. I'm sure they hid it from the lass. Their own sins caused the sad, disgraceful act of her being abducted. The

Lord is evidently chastising them, but the poor lass is innocent and has to suffer for their secret sin. They know not that I learned of their secret—their evil, horrific secret. How could someone so dear to me, to my parents, to the townsfolk be such a vicious monster and hide it? This abhorrent act is evil enough to avenge the victims, Lord. Where is Your goodness and mercy for the sake of righteousness? Where are You, Lord? I fear my disappointment in You is greater than my faith, and just look at what I have become. Do You not feel pity or shame in this wretched, painful crime of humanity? Is it not You who give us life and taketh it away? You taketh the wrong lives, Lord! I am furious, and You have hidden Yourself from my prayers, from my begging, and from my pleading prayers for righteous revenge. It's your fault, Lord. I will seek revenge, myself. A life for a life."

He looked up to the heavens, clenching his fists. Then, he lowered his head in disgust and crept into the shadows—crouching, planning his attack, and watching the window with wonder.

Talia walked up slowly to the window, peeking out, hesitant to stand up in front of it. She sensed something but could not justify her uneasiness.

What is this new fear that I am feeling? As shivers ran down her body, she rubbed her arms and hugged herself.

She finally garnered the courage to look out the window, but she saw nothing in the dark night. She wept, her tears escaping the bars and watering the weeds below.

Chatwin watched as the bewitching, sparkling path became even brighter. *Why is it getting brighter? Is there a meaning behind it?* He sucked in a deep breath, consumed by her recondite beauty. *Is she real?* He studied the sadness in her eyes. *I wonder how long she has been in isolation.*

Suddenly, Talia started singing while Chatwin watched and listened, confounded by the scene. Like something from a fairy tale, woodland creatures came out of the forest toward the house and stood still, listening.

Struggling with his plans, Chatwin's thoughts tortured him. What would his dear, sweet mother think of him now?

~

Percy walked into the room and aggressively asked, "You need to go to the loo?"

She shook her head yes.

He slipped a rope around her wrist like she was a pet being taken outside for a walk. "Move it!" he roared.

She followed him without speaking, noticing the broken furniture and Norman's black eyes and swollen face as she passed him. She glared at him with hatred, and he glared back.

After relieving herself, Percy took her back to her room. He pushed her into the room, and the bang of the door slamming caused her to jump.

"We'll be back in a week or so. Remember, I'll kill ye if you compromise this sale," Percy elaborated.

Chatwin heard the door slam and listened to the men recede into the distance. Just as he crept back up to the window, she came to the window and stared out into the forest. "Is anyone out there?" she asked bewildered. A gnawing suspicion tickled her brain as she scanned the area.

Chatwin sat motionless, wanting desperately to respond.

Suddenly, the old, wooden floor creaked as Harry walked back and forth to her door. Talia shot an anxious look out the window, begging someone to rescue her.

"I'll run in there and help you if he tries anything. I promise," he whispered.

Her silence was discomforting.

"I may not be your knight in shining armor, but I won't let him touch you. That much, I promise."

When the lights went out in the cottage, Chatwin realized that her guard had gone to bed. He breathed a sigh of relief.

Chatwin looked up in a tree, seeing the shiny eyes of a critter. When he realized it was a squirrel, he said, "Hey there, Buddy. Remember me? I'm heading back to my tent to see what supplies I have, but then I must return. She should be safe for a little while. The heavens have very graciously shined a path for me to follow, so I'll find my way back with no problem." He shook his head in disgust. "I'm literally talking to a squirrel. *Again*."

But as he walked away, his thoughts shifted. How many times did his butler suggest he needed therapy because he talked to himself so often? He had been through therapy before. It didn't work. Chatwin was stubborn, so therapy wasn't an option, but he did know that he couldn't afford to lose anyone dear to him ever again. When his butler fell ill, Chatwin couldn't catch his breath, and he came close to another mental breakdown. Then, after his butler recovered, Chatwin became distant to his staff, building a wall of protection around himself, should something horrible happen to any of them. His heart was turning to stone, and he couldn't seem to stop it.

∾

Talia curled up on the mattress but couldn't fall asleep. What else was there to do? She certainly didn't want to make any noise that would cause Harry to enter the room. He was too unstable. Something warm and fuzzy crawled up next to her. For a second, she was startled, but then she spotted her mouse. "Oh, hi, Tidbit." The mouse crawled into her cupped hands. She smiled with affection, kissing the top of Tidbit's head.

∾

Chatwin walked away with a sense of regret. Why didn't he just run in there and rescue her—and then turn around and kidnap her again? Why wait? His eyes stared at the ground as he walked in silence.

After shaking his head back and forth, he answered his own thoughts. "It doesn't matter, and I refuse to let her cause me regret. It is time to avenge the loss of life due to the folly of a man who was as close to being a family member as anyone could be without actually being born into the family. He truly is a beast, not I!"

Chapter Five

When Chatwin made it back to his tent, he surveyed the scene.

"What happened here? My supplies have been ransacked." He looked around and saw a fox hiding behind a tree. "I see you, you adorable thief. I'll leave some food behind when I leave, but right now, I have to pack everything up and hide it so that when I rescue—well, kidnap, actually, that enchanting creature, we can grab the stuff and leave." He pulled a handgun from his satchel and stuck it underneath his shirt, hoping he would never have to use it.

"Geez. Now, I'm talking to a fox." *You need help, buddy,* he thought. Chatwin waved goodbye to the fox and followed the heavenly-lit path back to the stone cabin.

When he walked up to the window, Tidbit heard the commotion and pulled away from Talia's grip, running back into his hole in the wall. Feeling Tidbit leave her hand, Talia awoke with a startle.

Her instincts drove her to the window.

As she stared out into the darkness, her body tingled from the top of her head to the bottom of her feet. She thought she sensed a presence, or was she imagining it? Suddenly, her eyes adjusted to the darkness, and a silhouette formed in the shadows.

"I know someone is out there. Please, come into the light. Show yourself."

Chatwin didn't move. *She will learn soon enough to never order me around.*

When Talia returned to bed, Chatwin crawled into his sleeping bag and stared at the night sky. The stars were bright and twinkling. The full moon shined just the right amount of light to make him feel safe. When he dozed off to sleep, her fairy-tale face haunted his mind.

~

The sweet, melodic chirps of songbirds resonated through the air. The moon was replaced by sprightly sunrays. Chatwin stretched, yawned, and sat up to listen.

Seeing that he was alone, Chatwin folded up his sleeping bag and walked around the stone cottage. In daylight, he noticed that the setting was a dump. Garbage littered the yard. Flowering vines twisted around the cottage's tower, draping along the roof.

"This place could be a beautiful, enchanting cottage if someone fixed it up. I'm going to snap some pictures of the disgusting way she had to live, should I need to remind her how grateful she should be for the luxury I will provide."

He peeked into the windows and saw Harry sleeping on the couch, slobber dribbling from his mouth, snoring like thunder. His chest rose up and down. Empty beer cans and whiskey bottles were lying everywhere.

"I can handle this guy. I don't think the door is locked. Why would you need to lock it out here?"

Just as Chatwin was about to open the door, Harry sat up. Cursing under his breath, he wobbled to the door. Chatwin jumped out of sight and watched. Harry walked into the

outhouse. When the door opened to it, the pong was overpow-
ering and disgusting, causing Chatwin to cover his nose and hold
his breath.

"Oh my. It smells like a manure farm. That poor, poor creature being subjected to these disgusting conditions," Chatwin
whispered.

He snapped a picture for more proof of the horrendous
living conditions. Then, he ran to her window. She was dressing,
so he turned around to give her privacy.

Talia walked up to the window and looked out, wondering
about the silhouette she saw last night. She cleared her throat.

Chatwin almost fell over. He stared at her hypnotically. *She
has some type of magical spell over me, and learning how to fight off that
spell will require a strong desire to succeed at my quest,* he thought.

The door slammed, and Talia ran back to her bed.

~

Chatwin hid outside the window and listened, peeking in where
he wouldn't be noticed. He heard creaking from Harry walking
on the rotting wooden floor.

The door opened.

"I'll bring you some breakfast, Princess."

He stared at her, looking up and down at her body, and then
ran out of the room.

"It looks like I may have to go forward with my plan sooner
than I originally anticipated. I'll have to rescue—or kidnap her
—oh, what's the difference at this point? Anyway, it's obvious he
is already having difficulty being around her. I can't let him harm
her."

~

Harry returned to the room with bread and butter, berries, a
pastry, and a cup of tea. Breakfast and lunch were the only meals

that were decent enough to eat. Supper usually consisted of some creature's brains and bat fangs or other things too horrible to picture—at least, that's what it looked like to her as she sifted through the mush.

This time, Harry didn't look at her. He put her tray down on the crate and left, slamming the door wordlessly.

Chatwin crept closer to the window and saw Talia eating. A little mouse sat next to her, eating a morsel of bread. A few birds landed on the iron bars, singing a sweet melody. She rewarded them by dropping pieces of bread outside the window.

It's like a Snow White or Sleeping Beauty movie coming to life. Don't let her enchant you, too, he warned himself. *You have a job to do.*

After fighting his conscience, he searched for something other than a gun to incapacitate the guard. His head nodded in approval at the club he found. Then he heard talking coming from her room. He ran back to keep an eye on the pervert.

Harry brought in a basin of water, and he stared at her as he sat it on the floor.

"Thank you," she said, putting the tray of dirty dishes in his hands.

Harry said nothing. He turned around, slamming the door on his way out. It slammed so hard, it rattled the window.

"I don't know if I can control myself much longer. She looks so delicious. I'm taking a walk. That should help," Harry mumbled with anger.

Chatwin hid as Harry walked past him. As soon as the guard was far enough away, Chatwin ran into the house and saw the huge, heavy block of wood across the door. He lifted the block of wood, but the sound of crunching debris startled him, so he ran out the door and hid. He watched Harry stumble into the cottage. Harry plopped down on the couch and fell back asleep in an instant.

Chatwin returned to Talia's window and watched her for nearly two hours while the guard slept. He had hoped the guard would leave again but decided to just have to confront the brute using the club he found. Just as he was about to open the door, Harry awoke and paced a trail back and forth between the couch and Talia's room.

"I'll kill that pervert if he tries anything," Chatwin said to himself. "I didn't think I cared, but watching the intensity of this situation is inhumane. I've never actually seen anyone be treated as evil and undeserving."

Chatwin backed up from the window but stayed close enough to listen.

He heard Talia's door open. "Why aren't you studying? How often have I told you the Sultan or Monarch—whatever he is— is expecting a beautiful, intelligent woman, not a wazzock one, like you."

Chatwin crept back up to the window and saw Harry holding his hand up to slap her, so he quickly stomped his feet on the ground to make enough noise to get the guard's attention.

Harry ran out of the room, bolted the door, and darted outside. "Must'a been some dumb animal."

Chapter Six

That evening, Harry walked into her room with dinner. He handed Talia some type of canned mush on a tray. She forced herself to sit up straight and imitate a smile. She dared not show ingratitude, or he would hit her. "Thank you," she said kindly while bile rose in her throat at the thought of eating what looked like mushed brains.

She stirred the tea, clinking the spoon nervously as he stared at her. He stood like a statue, casting a cold, evil stare. Finally, he walked out and slammed the door, but she heard him pacing back and forth. Creak, creak, creak. When the creaking vanished, an exhale of relief escaped her mouth.

The generator hummed, dispersing unpleasant gasoline fumes. Talia knew that it was time for him to get drunk and watch the telly.

Disgusted, she dropped the bowl of mush out the window, and some of it landed on Chatwin's head. He felt the mush between his fingers, cringed, and sniffed the sticky substance. *I swear that insect just fell over dead after eating this mush*, he thought. "One more day, and you can eat a plateful of French toast, Princess," he whispered.

Chatwin needed to find a place for mobile service. Since the brutes had mobiles, he knew there had to be service somewhere. He remembered seeing Harry walk out near the clearing, so he headed that way.

In the clearing, he dialed his assistant's number.

"Hello, your Lordship."

"Bertie, please bring an additional horse to my location. I'll leave my phone in this spot so that you can follow the GPS. This may be the only spot around here with service. Be swift, Bertie. I'm pretty sure I found her."

"Are you certain you want to do this, your Lordship?"

"Don't you turn on me now, Bertie. You have been with me since birth, and you have always known of my plans. I'm not a monster! This is the only way to get justice. Are you trustworthy, or do I need to discharge your services? If so, be gone then. Quickly."

"No, your Lordship. I will remain loyal, but my heart murmurs deep inside of me with sincere sadness. I won't deceive you, sir."

"Then make haste."

"Yes, your Lordship."

When the call ended, Bertie's head dropped, remembering how valiant, charming, and humorous Chatwin once was. *He was so intelligent, motivated, and handsome*, Bertie thought. *And now, the tragedy has changed him into someone I barely recognize.*

Chatwin glanced at his watch, and seeing that it was 11:00 p.m., he returned to the cottage. "Great. The brute is drunk as a skunk and watching a filthy movie. This can't be good. I better run and grab my club," Chatwin reasoned with himself.

After finding his club, Chatwin discovered that Harry was

sound asleep, with a beer bottle dangling from his hand. Chatwin looked in on Talia; she was also asleep, so he grabbed his sleeping bag.

~

The next morning, Chatwin woke, sitting up and rubbing his lower back.

Harry made breakfast and entered Talia's room as a sunray beamed through the window, illuminating her semi-sheer night-gown. Seeing his lustful intent, she climbed back in bed, covered her body with the tattered blanket, and said, "Good morning, Harry. Did you sleep well?"

He snarled, plopped the tray down, and left the room. At least he kept his distance. He didn't even bring her lunch that day.

That evening, Chatwin heard a pop from the tab of a beer can. He peeked in the window to see Harry drinking beer and watching sports, but then he reached for a sleazy DVD and inserted it into the VCR.

Chatwin needed a few more supplies before Bertie arrived, so he took off quickly to his tent so that he could return before Harry's drunkenness worsened.

Harry's demeanor was now that of anger, lustful necessity, and determination. He licked his lips repeatedly, swinging his knees back and forth rapidly. He was losing it.

While Chatwin was gone, Harry guzzled beer. Then, he paused his movie and yelled to himself. "She has tortured me all these years, thinking she's so smart that we can't touch her. She's been sneering at me, teasing me. That wretched tramp. You know what? There are more important things than money, and I'm about to prove it." His chest rose up and down with deep breaths.

He grabbed a lantern and stomped to her room. Hearing his

footsteps, Talia pulled the blanket up to her eyes and shut them tight.

"It's about time she gets what she deserves," Harry said to the closed door. He hurled open the door and walked in with a crazed look. He put the lantern down on the crate and crawled onto the mattress.

She screamed, and her eyes stretched open wide.

"Go ahead, Luv, scream. No one will hear you." He laughed with vigor and rubbed her arm. "Now be a good girl and be still." He bent down and kissed her arm, following the kisses up to her neck. His hands roamed over her body. Then he grabbed her hair and pulled her over to his grotesque mouth. He kissed her, pressing his lips so tightly against hers, pain severed through her lips.

It was her first kiss—and she was repulsed by it.

His breath smelled and tasted so bad, she likened it to kissing fish guts. She could barely contain the vomit rising in her throat. He slobbered down her chin and kissed down her neck, breathing rapidly. The smell of his disgusting body odor was the final blow. She vomited all over him in an uncontrollable, violent explosion.

He jumped back in disgust, but then, he raised his hand and slapped her so hard, she thought she would pass out. "You think that is going to stop me! Think again! What? Am I not good enough for a princess," he scoffed.

She covered her face with her hands, and her body curled into a ball. He instantly pulled her hands from her face and bent down so his face nearly touched hers. He scrunched his lips together with narrow, hateful eyes.

Talia let out another scream, and Harry ripped her gown. She tried to gather the torn nightgown around her to cover her breasts as he unzipped his pants. She screamed again.

Coming up the pathway, Chatwin heard the scream. The earth pounded beneath his feet as he ran into the house with the club and gun. Harry was so focused on his unhinged thoughts, he didn't even hear Chatwin enter the room.

With the power of Hercules, Chatwin bludgeoned Harry with the club, knocking him out cold. Then he pushed the attacker's unconscious body off her, rolling it onto the floor.

"You're okay now. Did he hurt you?" he asked, his voice soft and tender.

"Thankfully, you stopped him at the right time," she said. Unsure if she was hallucinating, she reached out and squeezed Chatwin's arm. "Are you real?" Talia whispered to herself.

"Come on. Get up. Throw on some clothes, and we'll get out of here," he said, noticing the bright red hand mark on her face. He turned his back to give her privacy.

"This nightgown and another gown is all I have to wear." She changed into the other gown anyway.

"Fine. Are you good to go, then?"

She nodded, and she watched him bring a bowl of water and food into the room, setting it on the crate.

"I don't know why I'm leaving sustenance for this brute. I should just let the hellion die of starvation. Anyway, let's go."

He turned to walk out the door, and Talia yelled, "Wait! Who are you? I can't leave Tidbit. I *won't* leave him! Please help me find him and his family. Usually, I throw bread down on the ground, and he comes out. I can't leave him!" she shouted with a quivering voice.

"I guess Tidbit is your mouse?"

She shyly nodded her head yes. "So, it wasn't in my head. You've been lurking in the shadows watching me?"

"Look. We don't have time to sit around and try to catch a mouse."

"He's not just a 'mouse'! He's the only friend I've had for years. I don't even know what year it is."

"I don't have time for this!" Chatwin grabbed her wrist and pulled her toward the door.

"Let go of me! I said I am not leaving without my mouse.

Who are you anyway? And why are you hiding your face from me? Are you a beast? A Monster? Maybe you're the Prince of Darkness?"

He held up his hand to warn her of an imminent slap and roared, "Shut your gob, and get moving!"

He lowered his hand without slapping her, but his words spewed so much animosity and intimidation that it felt like a mighty wind smacked her face. Then, realizing she would never see Tidbit again, she convulsed with tears.

With a hard voice, he asked, "Are you trying to provoke me?"

"No, sir. It's just that Tidbit has been my only companion. I love him so," she wailed.

"I told you to shut up about him!"

Once again, he threw his arm forward, pretending he was about to strike her. For a second, she looked deeply into his eyes. Then she screamed and passed out.

He looked over at the still-unconscious guard and then glanced at Talia, lying in a heap beside her bed. He shook his head, and tears formed in his eyes. He gently lifted her and placed her over one shoulder. *What have I become? Is it possible that I have truly transformed into a hideous beast?*

He carefully placed her on the mattress and fell to his knees, covering his face with his hands, sobbing passionately and sorrowfully.

"You've got to get it together," he said to himself.

He rose, lifted her over his shoulders, and walked out the door.

∽

"Your Lordship. I'm over here."

"Hold on to the horse so I can secure her. I fear she will try to escape."

"Your Lordship, what happened to her? Is she dead?"

"No. She passed out from fear."

Bertie's face teetered between horror, sorrow, and shame.

"I'll not have you look at me like I'm some sort of monster. Do I make myself clear?"

"Yes, your Lordship, but 'tis not I who looks at you that way. 'Tis yourself." Bertie proceeded forward. "I have tents set up. We should be at that location soon."

"Wait," Chatwin said, pausing and running his hand through his hair. "Do you think you could find your way back to the tents from this cottage? I need you to uh... to trap her pet mouse—and it has a family. She was quite upset about leaving them."

Bertie smiled.

"Don't smile. I'm sticking with the plan. I just need to keep her content so she'll be compliant."

"Aye, your Lordship. I will retrieve the mice. Here is your mobile." Bertie handed him the phone and smiled again.

Talia opened her eyes and looked around, trying to figure out where she was and what had happened to her. She glanced down at the horse. As she turned to glance at her new captor, she sucked in a quiet gasp. Their eyes met. Trembling at his power over her, she flinched with fear.

"I'm not going to hurt you," he said with annoyance. "We will stop and rest shortly."

"Where are you taking me?"

"Obviously, I am not going to divulge that tidbit of information."

"Tidbit!" She started sobbing again.

"Don't make me shut you up! Do you hear me?" he roared.

She collected her composure and asked, "How far do we have to travel?"

"Not far."

"Do you mind if I pray?" she asked.

"Whatever you wish," he replied.

She nodded, closed her eyes, and said, "Dear God, do You hate me so that You have sacrificed me to Satan himself? What have I ever done to deserve this, dear Lord?" She opened her eyes and looked up toward heaven. "Why not take my life? That would be more humane than allowing me to suffer at the hands of Satan. Am I not the same soul, in years of soliloquy, who questioned my very existence? Do you laugh at my dire, lonely, pathetic request for death? 'Death, where is thy sting?' I surrender my soul this very day into Your hands, My Lord and Savior, and I vow to reject your enemy. I will spit in the beguiling face of the Prince of Darkness." She looked at Chatwin with deep, scornful hate.

"Well, that was an eye-opening statement. You think of me as Satan himself, do you? That is a bit of an exaggeration, don't you think?" He snorted with amusement.

"I fail to see humor in this situation."

Just then, Bertie rode toward her on his horse. As the horse trotted beside them, he pressed a canvas bag into her hands. "Here you go, Miss. Be gentle."

She looked curiously at Bertie and gently opened the bag. Her eyes and mouth popped open wide, and tears of happiness trailed down her cheeks. "Tidbit. My Tidbit." The mouse looked agitated, so she said, "Don't worry, my friend. I am here, and I promise to keep you and your family safe."

Chatwin kept his face morose as he watched her encounter with the mouse. *She's perfect,* he thought. *Could she be an angel sent from heaven above?*

"Thank you. Thank you so much," Talia remarked. She glanced at her captor, but his dark gaze was unreadable.

Bertie, whose horse was still trotting beside them, said, "It took me longer than I thought to follow your friend and capture them all, Miss."

Chatwin glared at Bertie and said, "Yes, you're right. It took way too long!" Then, he glanced at Talia and noticed her feet, which were swollen and peppered with angry cuts. He pulled back on his reins. "Holt!"

His horse came to a stop, and Bertie stopped beside him. "What is it—"

Before Bertie could finish his sentence, Chatwin raised his hand to silence him. Then, he whispered in his ear, "I do not want her to know me. Just answer yes, sir, please."

"Aye, your—I mean, yes, sir."

Talia stared at them with curiosity, trying to hear the conversation.

"Bertie, we need to attend to the lass' medical needs. Do you have any bandages and ointment in your supplies?"

"Aye, I do in the tent. We'll be there shortly."

"Excuse me, but do you think it wise that we stop anywhere, sir?" Talia asked. "If Harry escapes my room, he'll kill us all. My feet will be fine."

"The brute won't get out. He's not strong enough to break those iron bars loose—at least not for a long time."

"Are you sure? I can't go back there. I can't!"

"We are safe. *You* are safe. We're almost to the camp where Bertie set up the tent. You need some sleep before we finish our journey. I'll keep watch. As for that scoundrel, I will bring the authorities out here, and we'll put a stop to their evil plan once and for all."

"So I am rescued? You will return me to my family?"

"Not exactly," he replied.

"Then, I was correct. You *are* the Prince of Darkness. You did not rescue me. You just stole me for your *own* benefit. If you contact the authorities, won't they also consider your actions a crime?"

"Absolutely. I will arrange for an anonymous message to be left outside Scotland Yard. I will stop the people who abducted you."

"That's nice. Who will stop you?" she grumbled under her breath.

"Gordon Bennett, woman! You would be best to keep your gob shut. I will offer you luxury, at least, and food fit for a queen —or shall I rephrase that statement to say, 'princess'?"

"I'm *not* a princess. They only called me a princess because I was off-limits. It wasn't meant in any form of prestige, believe me. Besides, I would live in squalor and eat mush the rest of my life if it meant I could be with my family and friends again."

"You would be wise to shut your gob. Not another word from you!"

She stuck her head up high and held a defiant stare.

At the campsite, Bertie attended to her medical needs while Chatwin attended to calls and e-mails. When he returned, Talia was sitting around a fire while Bertie prepared dinner. Chatwin watched as Bertie gave the mice food and water. When Talia started singing, the mice looked happy. *How does she charm animals so?* Chatwin looked at Bertie, and he, too, looked joyful as well. *She's already gotten to Bertie,* he thought.

Chatwin approached the fire and sat on a log before the flames. "It smells delicious. Bertie, you always perform magic with food. Thank you."

"You're welcome, your—sir."

Talia glanced at Bertie and then glanced at the beastly man. Their dynamic was puzzling. Bertie seemed kind, caring, and thoughtful—such an inverse from his lordship, but Bertie acted *fond* of his boss. *How curious! Though he is hard to read, he seems to have a soft spot for Bertie. I don't get it. I don't get any of it.*

"If you don't mind, I think I need to get some sleep. I didn't think I would feel this tired, but I am exhausted. I could sleep for days," Talia said politely.

"Good to go. You'll need your rest. We'll leave at daybreak."

"I can't get my brain to realize I'm really free from those monsters. Well, I guess I'm not really free, but at least Bertie seems to like having me around. Oh, but I really miss my family, and Adelaide, our housekeeper, and Twiggly Wigglesbottom, our butler." She suddenly broke out into sobs.

Chatwin stood and looked away, "Bertie, get the lady situated in her tent. I must tend to the horses." He walked toward the horse and then turned back to look at her. "Look. I promise you I will never let anyone hurt you again. I understand why you don't believe me, but hurting you was never my intention."

Talia wiped her tears and looked at him defiantly. "Let's see, you rescued me from my abductors, and then you turned around and captured me, yourself. I'm not feeling overly confident about your proclamation of safety. How much money do you intend to get for me?"

"None. As we get to my manor, I will send the authorities back to that dreadful cottage in the forest. That's all you need to know. Now, I have nothing more to say. Bertie, close the tent up, and I'll stand guard."

"Yes, sir."

Chapter Seven

After breakfast, they headed out on their journey. Even though Talia hadn't actually been rescued, she felt jovial, and she couldn't discern why. She stole furtive glances at Chatwin, wondering if he would prove to be evil. *Maybe I'm happy because Bertie is so kind*, she thought. She glanced at her abductor again. Though he acted indifferent, her instincts told her that he cared about her needs.

She peered into her bag at Tidbit and his family. *He obviously told Bertie to retrieve Tidbit. Maybe, just maybe, he will show me kindness.* She looked around, smiled, and sniffed the air. *Ahhh. But I am outside—and free from that dungeon. So, whatever happens from here on out, today is a glorious day.*

She smelled the familiar scents of violets and primrose floating in the breeze. The wind tickled her face, blowing hair across her eyes while the sun warmed her face. And her feet! Oh, how they felt wonderful. She wiggled her toes. *No more stomping through stones and rubble to the outhouse.*

Chatwin glanced over and noticed the smile on her face. Almost instinctively, he smiled, but then he turned his head, and his grin disappeared.

"How much farther do we have to go?" Talia asked.

"We should be home just before twilight."

"Will we be able to stop and water the horses? They must be thirsty and tired."

He wanted to be annoyed, but he found himself entranced by her engaging quiddity. *Why, oh, why couldn't she act like some rich, spoiled brat! No. She has to be charming and kind, unselfish.*

"Yes, of course, we will stop soon. I do have a question for you, though. It seems that you are well-versed in knowledge, and yet, you've been abducted for, I think, about five years with no schooling."

"Fortunately, I was made to study so I wouldn't be a wazzock. They planned to sell me to a sultan who wanted a beautiful, intelligent bride, or so I was told. I was given plenty of schoolbooks to help me learn during my *delightful* stay at the cottage in the forest. I am not, however, well-versed in current affairs. Any chance you would update me on current events?"

"I don't know if that is wise. When we get home and get you settled in, however, I will give it some thought."

You are not taking me home—not to my home, anyway, she thought. *Perhaps I should pay close attention to him to see how I can earn his trust. Maybe he'll reduce my sentence if I remain on good behavior, or maybe I can get him to let down his guard and escape, somehow.*

"Please don't take this the wrong way, sir," she said, "but why do you look like Rip Van Winkle? With all that hair and your scraggly beard? And you're always covering your face with a hoodie. Perhaps you are a vampire. Is it because you can't look into the light that ye may possibly burn up?" Her eyes narrowed with a smug tilt of her head.

"My looks are none of your concern."

"Are you a criminal in hiding?"

He took a deep breath. "You would do well to quit talking."

Bertie cleared his throat to get her attention. She looked at him, and he shook his head, indicating that she should stop questioning him. *Message received.*

∼

They were eating lunch while the horses rested when they heard voices in the distance.

"Quick, Bertie, take the horses and the princess and hide. I'll handle the rest."

"Aye," Bertie replied, herding Talia and the horses away.

When the strangers approached, Chatwin waved at them and said, "Good day, sirs."

"Good day. What would you be doing out in the wilderness by yourself?" one of the strangers asked.

∼

From her hiding spot, Talia strained to hear the conversation. Suddenly, she started trembling.

"Miss, what is it?"

"The Sultan. I heard the name of the Sultan. These are the people who plan to purchase me."

Bertie patted her arm. "No worries. The good sir will protect you and get them to move forward. You will see."

∼

"I am a wilderness photographer," Chatwin told the stranger. "Care to see some of my photographs?"

"Why not?" the man replied cautiously.

The rest of his group stood quietly as Chatwin passed around his photos.

"These are impressive," the stranger said. "Thank you for sharing them with us, but we must be on our way now."

Chatwin watched them trot away on their horses. When he could no longer see them, he said, "You can come out now. The coast is clear. Bertie, we need to move quickly before they reach their destination. Are we good to go?"

"Aye, we are good, sir."

∿

Talia was amazed that he let her ride her own horse. *I could just gallop away,* she thought. *But then, where would I go, and what if I run into the men who were supposed to purchase me?*

Bertie had told her that they were close to the manor, and now, he and the good sir whispered in seriousness. Talia guided her horse closer and leaned in toward them to eavesdrop on the conversation. Just then, a powerful wave crashed just feet away from her. She gasped and looked at waves crashing against the nearby cliffs.

Chatwin laughed. "Ah. That's what you get for trying to eavesdrop."

She shot him an insolent glare.

"No worries, Lass. We are close to the sea, but we're far enough away from the raging waves to be safe."

She nodded, though she wasn't sure she believed him. As dusk approached, she tried to focus on the scene ahead—a tall wall of trees. She couldn't make anything out beyond the trees, but soon, they trotted into the forest, and behind a cluster of trees, a driveway of cobblestones appeared. Still, she saw no visible structures indicating they were close to his manor. Then, as if appearing from nowhere, she saw a tall, iron gate, which opened.

As they passed through it, she thought, *Why do I feel excited? I'm a prisoner, after all.*

She watched as Chatwin removed an electronic device. Suddenly, the gate closed behind them, and the fence came alive with a loud buzzing sound.

A high-voltage fence? Well, that definitely denigrates my escape plan. She felt a moment of despair, but then she scanned the grounds ahead, and she smiled, delighted by the most enchanting place she had ever seen. The stone manor—or, more accurately, the castle—with a tower and all— was magnificently beautiful, with flowering vines stretching across the roof and encircling the tower. The grounds were impeccably attended to with lush green trees, flowering trees, willow trees, and every variety of flower she could imagine. She was taken aback at the number of lilies surrounding the estate.

It's beautiful, but why are there so many lilies? It was as though the castle was built by her own hands, just the way she imagined her dream home. Then she saw it. Iron bars covered the floor-to-ceiling windows. Her smile vanished, and she sighed. *Just another prison.*

"Your home is most beautiful," she commented out of courtesy, pulling the hood of the cape he gave her over her head. She heard thunder in the distance as a light drizzle fell. The sound of crashing waves startled her, and she jerked.

"Thank you. Are you okay? You appear to have a frightened face."

"Oh. I heard crashing waves, and it startled me. We must be close to the sea." She sniffed. "Just as I thought. I can smell the brininess."

"Aye. It seems that the sea is at war with my estate. It used to be calmer than this, but I must have offended it somehow."

What a surprise, she thought sarcastically. "Why is it that horses are your chosen way to travel?" She patted the horse's neck affectionately.

"No vehicle would have made it through the dangerous areas we traversed. Only a horse could maneuver through."

She nodded. "I'm sure you will be well taken care of for your exhausting struggles through this treacherous terrain, sweet pony," she said as she rubbed the horse's neck.

When they stopped before the manor, some caregivers arrived and took the horses to the stable. Talia stood before the enormous estate, staring up at it.

"Bertie will show you to your room. Until I can trust that you won't be childish enough to try and escape, you will be confined to your room and only allowed out for meals," Chatwin said.

She twitched nervously and dropped her head. Bertie touched her arm lightly. "It's okay, Miss. Follow me."

She kept her head down as she followed Bertie, ignoring the castle's interior.

When Bertie said, "Here we are, Miss. These will be your quarters." She looked up, and her face lit up with a smile.

It was like her own private home.

"There are three levels," Bertie told her.

The downstairs level had a living room and kitchen area.

"Is that a terrace?" she asked Bertie.

"Yes. Each floor has a terrace."

Her eyes lit up briefly, but she was dismayed to see that iron cages enclosed the promenades. *I may not be able to escape, but at least I can go outside and smell the fresh air,* she thought.

She held her breath as she examined the exquisite tapestries and paintings dispersed throughout the area. She noticed Persian rugs and custom-made craftsman furniture.

"Would you like to see the second level, Ma'am?" Bertie asked.

He escorted her to the second floor, and her mouth opened wide, seeing the silk bedding, fluffy pillows, and delicate fabrics that covered the room in splendor. Long, silky curtains blew in the breeze.

"You may change clothes when you are ready, Miss. You'll find new attire in the wardrobe," Bertie told her.

When she walked over to the wardrobe and pulled the doors open, her heart sank. She saw outfits were for every occasion. It contained every style of shoe, with dresses and gowns, with shorts, tops, slacks, and even hair scrunches.

Bertie approached a dresser and pulled open a thin drawer. "This remote will give you access to the jewelry bureau," he said.

With a push of a button, the drawers opened, and she saw sparkling jewels, gold, and silver.

"I can wear these?" she asked hesitantly.

"Of course, Ma'am. Let me show you the restroom." He opened the doors to a gigantic bathroom.

She froze. It was fit for a queen. Seeing the deep, luxurious bathtub, she said, "Bertie, would it be possible for me to take a bath now?"

"I'm sorry, Miss, but I've been instructed to give you the entire tour. We must finish first. Please hold on a minute." He pulled a mobile out of his pocket and sent a text. "Now, if you would follow me, I'll show you the third level."

They walked up the third-floor steps, and she flinched in shock when she entered the space. "My own personal library and media room?"

"Yes. Though, the good sir will not allow Internet or live telly access, so it *is* limited. There is, however, a huge selection of current and older movies and television shows. Same with music. You have all the current and oldies you would ever want."

She picked up a Herman's Hermits album and smiled. "I just love these guys. I'll never quit listening to them." Then she picked up a DVD of the *Poldark* series. "My mother started watching this right before my first kidnapping."

She looked at Bertie with an awkward stare. He donned a sympathetic smile.

"The story looks so intriguing. I can't wait to watch it. Oh, look—*Father Brown* and *Downton Abbey*. *Sanditon*? I never heard of it. It's from a Jane Austin novel?"

"Yes. Apparently, this series is from a book she never completed. The ending is almost frustrating."

"I can't wait to watch it. Not to mention," she said, pointing to a character, "he is very pleasing to the eyes."

"Ah, yes. That seems to be the reaction from women."

"Shall I tell the good sir you are pleased, ma'am?"

She looked around and saw vases of exquisite flowers filling the tower. She twirled around, inhaling the aroma of the flowers. "Yes. I am pleased, Bertie," she said when suddenly, her bag shook. "Oh, Tidbit, I forgot about you. Bertie, where may I put them?"

"If you walk out onto the terrace, you'll see an appropriate place for them. The good sir called ahead of time to set this up. He wants you to be most comfortable and happy here."

She looked confused. "He doesn't really seem to care if I'm happy."

"Oh, come now, Miss Talia. He wouldn't have gone to all this trouble if he didn't want you to be happy."

"Well, if you say so," she replied. She stepped onto the terrace and saw a large cage for the mice with a house. She quickly placed the mice in the cage. "Look at your new home. Isn't it beautiful?" The mice ran around like they were as excited as she looked about their surroundings.

"Madam, if you'll notice, the cage will allow the mice to travel down the built-in stairs to every level of the tower. They will be able to roam without escaping, and they won't have to worry about predators such as cats and hawks. I do need you to know, though, that the good sir is having me take them to the veterinary surgeon at the brink of dawn to make it so they can no longer breed. They'll be in good care and return shortly after."

"That makes sense. Please express my utmost appreciation to—to the Lordship? Excuse me for being so blunt, but he most certainly is not my lord, and I refuse to call him as such. So, what do I call him?"

"I would just call him sir—good sir."

"I don't know if I can stomach the 'good' part of that. This—" she spread her hands out, "is wonderful, but he still has taken away my chance of freedom and happiness, along with the opportunity to reconnect with my family and friends."

A tear slipped down her face. It glistened.

"Aye, Miss. I see your point."

There was a knock at the door. A cheerful, globose-shaped

woman walked in with fresh towels. "Good day, Miss. I will fill your bath. Any preference for bath salts?"

"No. I do not have a preference. Thank you. But, please, you don't have to fix me a bath. I can certainly do that myself. I'm sure you have much more pressing jobs than waiting on me. Please. Having someone waiting on me makes me feel a little uncomfortable."

"Aye, miss, but that is what the Lordship hired me specifically to do. If I am not allowed to be your personal maid, he will no longer need my services. This job is beneficial to my well-being, and no one could ask for better living accommodations. Please, miss. I very much would like to stay here."

"Of course. I am just not used to being waited on. Please excuse me. Even our housekeeper, Adelaide, used to try and wait on me, but she gave up, so it is not personal. But I assure you I'll do whatever you need to keep this job. Besides, I could certainly use a woman to talk with. Bertie is wonderful, but sometimes a girl just needs another woman around."

"Aye. Thank you, Miss. I am more than happy to be at your disposal anytime, day or evening. Now, I will set up a bath so you can have a nice long soak. Soon after, supper will be served."

"What are we having for supper?"

"I believe tonight's menu includes cottage pie, with fresh greens and spotted dog for dessert."

"What do I call you, Miss?" Talia asked.

"You may call me Poppy."

"Lovely name. Poppy, I can't wait for supper. If you only knew how long it has been since I had anything so delightful to eat."

"Aye, miss. That, I was told. Now, off into the bath for you."

"This will be the first bath I've had in five years."

"Oh, my, child. I am certain that you may need an extensive amount of time to bathe then. I'll keep supper warm."

"That will be divine. Thank you so much." She hugged Poppy and ran to the washroom.

Covered with suds, Talia scrubbed all the way down to the hypodermis layers. She hummed a sweet tune while scrubbing her skin almost raw. She didn't know if she would ever feel truly clean and refreshed, but still, the bath was magnificent. Her eyes closed, and she sunk down in the warm water with pleasure. And the fragrance, oh, how it lulled her into relaxation.

After her bath, she dressed, and when her stomach rumbled, she realized she was starving. "I'm so hungry that my mouth won't quit watering just thinking about supper."

"Knock, knock," Polly said, entering the room with a tray full of heaven.

Talia froze and sniffed the air. "Have I died and gone to heaven? I can't wait another moment." She ate with heartfelt gratitude, thanking God for His goodness. "Is there any chance you could take me to the kitchen to thank the chef? I don't want to get you in trouble, so be honest."

"I think that will be okay. But beware, the chef is quite a grump." Poppy's lip curved on one side. "Follow me, but then we must get you back to the tower."

As they walked, Talia eagerly surveyed each room, her eyes planting on each painting she passed. She noticed the costly fabric of the curtains and the expensive rugs.

"Is that a Chesterfield sofa?" she asked.

"Why, yes, it is. It belonged to the Lordship's mother."

Her head turned in every direction at the beauty of the manor. When they arrived in the immaculate kitchen with state-of-the-art appliances, her eyes scanned the floor, and she could see her reflection on the pristine porcelain stone tile.

Admiring the floor, lost in thought, Poppy cleared her throat. She looked up to see the chef preparing a very aromatic tea.

"My dear, this is Chef Charles. Charles, this is Talia."

She quickly approached him and kissed his cheek. "Nice to meet you."

His mouth dropped, and he stood still.

Poppy covered her hand over her escaped laugh, not wanting to further engage his fury.

"Dear Sir, that supper was magnificent. Ye had to have a host of heavenly angels to assist you, as the flavors were out of this world." She smiled brightly.

Still flabbergasted, the chef merely nodded.

As Poppy escorted her out of the kitchen, the chef tilted his head, and the corner of his lips turned up in a small smile.

Chapter Eight

T alia adjusted to her new life. Each evening, she stood on the terrace and stared at the cliffs—and every night, she saw him there, his terrifying form, standing powerfully, overlooking the highest peak.

Watching his silhouette on the rocky terrain, he became a beast in her thoughts.

In the setting of dark, shaded trees, she could make out wolf's ears, or something like it in his shadowy figure. The mere presence of his outline seemed arrogant, and she imagined that his power controlled the sun, moon, and stars.

But he didn't have power over the sea. That, she could see. "I fear the beast has made the sea his foe. I'll even bet his arrogance spiked an ongoing battle between them," she murmured aloud as the waves crashed and churned in turmoil, pounding against the cliffs.

Sometimes she would imagine the waves consuming him, sucking him and his arrogance into the sea. She could almost see him fall to his death, his body being tossed to and fro, never to resurface—never to command his kingdom again—and finally setting her free.

And yet, she still felt an unexplained sadness for him. Oh,

how she wanted to hate him, but when she envisioned his death, she only felt guilt, which she attributed to her relationship with the Lord, so she often sent up prayers for forgiveness.

Talia grew fond of Poppy and Bertie, but her heart was still lonely. Even though their lordship kept her captive, they were a loyal bunch who would not speak ill about their Lordship, and they would not divulge any personal information about him. *What type of spell does he have over them?* she often wondered. But in her heart, she felt like there was more to it than that. She sensed that they liked him and felt admiration for their lord. She finally concluded that they were loyal to him out of love and gratitude—not fear or pity. They genuinely loved this beastly person. But how? But why?

∽

A few nights earlier, Talia noticed that her door could be unlocked from either side—if she only had the key. All staff members had keys, so she watched them closely, paying attention to their routines.

That evening, Talia managed to steal the chef's set of keys after she asked him to give her a warm glass of milk to calm her nerves. Her act of deceit caused her indescribable guilt, but she needed information.

Later that night, when Poppy unlocked the door to her room, Talia was hiding behind a dresser, holding a remote that controlled a recorder she had placed in the washroom. She hit play on the remote, and her voice rang out from the bathroom. "I'm in the loo, Poppy. My stomach is not feeling too well. Please leave the milk at my bedside, and I'll drink it before I fall asleep. I am in no mood for company, I fear. Goodnight, sweet Poppy."

"Okay, you poor dear. Please sleep tight."

After Poppy closed the door, Talia waited a few minutes and then fumbled with her stolen key to find the correct one. When she unlocked the door, she peered outside to ensure no one was in the hallway. Then, she quietly tiptoed down the stairs, carefully looking around her. All was quiet.

She knew from the staff that the good sir had gone on another job-related trip. She hadn't spoken to him in a month, but she wondered why he kept her captive if he didn't plan on intimidating her, torturing her, or treating her like the captive she really was. He ate dinner in his chambers every evening.

She tip-toed through the manor and thought, *What is so special about his dumb room? I will find out for myself.*

She crept up the stairs leading to his room. Before she could search for the correct key to unlock the door, she heard footsteps. She hurriedly hid behind the thick, velvet curtain outside of his door. She listened closely and heard the footsteps fade away. Then she heard the door to the servants' chambers open and close, so she peeked her eyes out around the curtain. Certain she was alone again, she searched for the right key to open the good sir's door.

On the fourth try, she turned the key in the lock, and it clicked. The noise made her jump, and she looked around to make sure no one heard. Then, she took a deep breath and stepped inside the beast's chambers. With trembling fingers, she silently closed the door behind her. Her whole body shook in fear. A branch scraped against the window, and she covered her mouth to keep from screaming in fear. She looked around the dark room and wondered, *What will I find? Bones? Skulls? What secrets does he hold?*

"Why won't he reveal his face? Just what is he hiding?" she whispered, stuttering the words. *Maybe he is a vampire.* She had never actually seen his face, but she *did* see his eyes, and they were intense, even secretive. *I've never seen him in the light of day,* she thought. *Goodness. What atrocities will I stumble upon? Maybe this was a foolish move.*

The first room was his study. She sniffed the air, expecting to detect the pungent odor of decaying bodies. Surprisingly, the air smelled normal—sweet, even. She ran her hand across the wood paneling, noticing its rich tone. She observed the masculine table and chairs made out of Albobenga wood. *This furniture is well made and looks quite expensive.*

She saw a door to the left and a door to the right. Her hand trembled as she slowly turned the handle on the door to the left. She tiptoed into a homey sitting room with a couch made of expensive-looking wood with dark gold cushions that felt like feathers as she sunk into it. Her hands moved over the fabric, and she reclined against the back cushions. *This is dreamy. I could sleep on this couch.* She found it odd that she saw no portraits or pictures or knickknacks. *Odd. This is supposed to be his personal space.*

Further back, she spotted a kitchenette, which was small and cozy with quality appliances, but it only held a small table with one chair. *How lonely.*

Every room was immaculate. She carefully opened the door to the study and looked around before entering back through it. She passed by the desk and saw a computer! *Oh my gosh! If I could only remember my Mum's email address.* She decided that she didn't have time to use the computer. *No, I need to get some information first. I can always come back the next time he goes on a trip.*

She passed a bar section with elegant decanters that were empty. *No liquor?* She looked at the door on the right of the study, knowing it must be his bedroom.

She held her hands to her mouth and sucked in a deep breath. With wide eyes, she turned the doorknob and entered his bedroom, scanning the room with one thing on her mind—a coffin.

"No coffin!"

She wiped beads of sweat from her forehead. The room was tastefully decorated and spotless. The expensive, masculine bedding and the strong, custom-crafted furniture were exactly what she envisioned his room to look like—except for the coffin she had expected to find. Then, a painting caught her eye. It was a painting of a family: a father, a mother, and a baby boy. *Hmmmm. I wonder if that was his family.* She started to walk away but froze and returned to the portrait. As if hypnotized, she walked toward the picture. The eyes of the baby boy seemed familiar to her. *It looks like his eyes, except they feel happy and loving. Wait! Where have I seen these people before? I think I know them, but I can't remember...*

Suddenly, she heard footsteps and a low, grumbling voice. She hid just as the door hurled open with a whoosh, smashing into the wall behind it.

"Who left my door unlocked?"

Talia's heart pounded through her chest. What would he do if he found her?

"I can't believe I left without my notes. Call and inform them that I will arrive late—please."

She heard Bertie reply, "Yes, sir."

Then she heard him storm out of the room, slamming the door shut behind him. A few seconds later, she heard the lock click in place.

She tiptoed to the window and peered outside. A chauffeur held the Bentley car door open as the beastly man entered. He had on a cape, the hood covering his face, as usual. As they zoomed off, she decided to continue with the search.

She found no bones, no pieces of fur—nothing! No evidence of a beast. She picked up a bottle of men's cologne, *Tom Ford*, private blend. "This looks quite expensive," she whispered. When she passed by a bookshelf, she tilted her head upwards and stood in thought. *Maybe there is a secret entrance to a secret room.* She pulled the books back, feeling around the wall. A door opened when she accidentally touched a nail protruding from the wood. She gasped and put both hands over her mouth. *Maybe the bedroom is a decoy, and his coffin is down in this dark chamber.*

She took one shaky step after the next, down a set of stairs leading her to another door. She put her hand on the doorknob and was about to turn it when she looked up and noticed an alarm at the top of the door. She pulled her hand away and instead walked to a set of windows adjacent to the door. She pulled the curtains back from the window and peered through. The door led outside! *A secret escape and entrance for the vampire, but where is his coffin?*

Frustrated, she walked quietly back up the stairs and carefully poked her head inside his room. It was safe.

She resumed her search and discovered that his closet must have been three times the size of her bedroom in her parents' house. She felt the fabric of his expensive-looking suits. One section had a whole row of hoodies. Everything was in its place, and she saw nothing unusual. At the end of the closet, she discovered an entrance to a workout room with all the exercise equipment one would ever need. Fingers pinched her nose together because the disinfectant smell was strong.

"Darn. He appears to be human." Walking past the bed, she noticed several photographs on his dresser. She picked up the first frame. "Grandparents." The next photograph must have been of his parents when they were young, but both were in black and white and appeared dated.

"Hhhh!" she gasped out loud, then covered her mouth. She grabbed the last photograph with both hands. The last photograph was of a *WOLF!*

"Why would he have a photograph of a wolf? Maybe he's a werewolf, not a vampire. He *does* like to roar."

Then she heard the sounds of frantic voices. She listened, walking quietly toward the exit door.

"Talia is not answering me. Should I go in without her consent? I promised never to invade her privacy," Poppy said tremulously.

"My dear, just give her a moment. Maybe she is in the loo or upstairs in the library.

Give her a few moments and try again. Please don't allow yourself such turmoil," Bertie commented.

"I need to get back into my room." Talia exited the good sir's room cautiously and as quietly as a mouse. Avoiding the staff, she made it back to her room without being seen, but as she plopped down on the bed, she realized that she had dropped the keys somewhere in her haste to return to her quarters!

"Oh my. I better hide my tape recorder. I forgot to look for mail on his desk. If I had done that, I would at least know his name, and I could've found out this address. Drats. I didn't learn anything, really." She sighed.

A knock came at the door. "Talia, dear, are you all right?"

"Yes, Poppy. I have been sound asleep."

"I'm so sorry to disturb you. I was just worried about you."

"Thank you for that, but I'm going back to sleep. You just go and do something for yourself—you and Bertie. You both deserve some time to yourselves."

"Thank you. I believe I will watch some telly. Good evening, then."

I made it, but I still need answers. I'll find them one way or the other, Talia thought.

Chapter Nine

The next evening at dinner, Talia stood up and boldly said, "I would like to arrange a meeting with the beast —the Prince of Darkness."

The staff looked at her like snakes were growing out of her head.

"I will not take no for an answer. If he refuses, I will not eat another bite until such time as he honors me with his *royal* presence." She crossed her arms and stood tall.

"Now, now. Don't get yourself in a tizzy, Lass. The beast, as you refer to him, is quite a busy man," Poppy said.

"Oh, so he is a man, then. Not a beast?"

"Oh, Lass, I may not speak of him. I'm sorry. I really am sorry."

"Poppy, I insist on a word. I will not eat another bite until then. Excuse my rudeness, but I WISH TO SPEAK TO THE BEAST OR HIS HIGHNESS OR HIS JERKINESS, whatever the heck you call him." She sat back down, her body straight, her arms crossed, and her face defiant.

Suddenly, she heard a voice reply, "And just what would you dare say to him, Princess?"

She looked up to see the beast himself, with his back facing her.

"Would you mind facing me like a gentleman?"

"Yes, I would mind. You have one minute to speak your mind before I leave this room."

She found his demanding persona contumelious.

"Are you too proud to speak with the prisoners, or are you so hideous that my heart will stop beating at the sight of you? I have only to conclude that you *are* a beast! Or maybe that hoodie hides your horns, Prince of Darkness."

Before he could reply, thunder roared, and lightning crashed to the ground. She screamed in terror. *Did he summon the thunder and lightning?*

"There, there, Miss. It is just a rainstorm," he said, his back still to her. "Now, I must get back to work."

"I will not stand for this! Why have you captured me? For sport, like some deranged hunting trophy? Why keep me here if you refuse to spend time with me? Or maybe you look upon *me* as some type of ugly beast. Is that it? Does my hideous sight cause too much fear for you to look upon? What is it?"

"You're overreacting, and I refuse to succumb to your childish ways. However, do you really want to spend time with a beast, as you describe me? How odd. Which is it? Am I a beast, or am I the Prince of Darkness?"

He began to walk out of the room.

In a rage, she jumped up and ran out of the room toward the front door. "I would rather die than live another day at the hands of a selfish beast."

The guard at the door ran toward her, and somehow, she maneuvered him away from the door. Then she crashed through the doorway into the tumultuous storm, heading for the gate.

Chatwin ran after her. She was quick and fast, but he was faster. He grabbed her just before she reached the gate. He lifted her up off her feet, and she pounded his chest.

Her hands ached as it felt like she was hammering steel and stone. "I hate you! I hate you so much! Let me die. I beg you. This isn't a life for anyone. I would rather die."

Lightning flashed, and she mistook the reflection of lightning for flames in his eyes.

His eyes were filled with intensity and hate—nothing like the happy eyes of the boy in the family photograph. He opened his mouth to speak just as it thundered, and she mistook that, too, for a roar. She was so scared, she passed out.

Chatwin sighed and carried her to the castle.

The pounding raindrops soaked her gown, causing the silky, thin fabric to cling to her body. She was no longer frail and sickly, he noticed.

Chatwin swallowed hard. He had to take his eyes off her to control the shameful thoughts. Even in the rain, her skin and hair glistened like the dew of heaven. He couldn't make sense of it.

He handed Talia to the guard, who was breathing heavily from exhaustion and rattled nerves. "Take her upstairs to her room. Poppy, change her into dry clothing, and she is *not* permitted to leave her room for a week—*or longer*. I will not permit her to commit suicide on my watch."

"Your Lordship, don't you..."

"Don't you say it! You knew the plan from the beginning."

As Poppy dressed Talia, she opened her eyes. Everyone in the castle could hear the Lordship's savage roar and screams emanating from his room as glass and furniture crashed against the walls and floor.

Talia grabbed Poppy and held on to her with such fear that Poppy couldn't control her trembling body in her arms.

∿

The next morning, after coming to his senses, Chatwin came down to breakfast with a hood covering his face and sunglasses over his eyes.

"Will it make you happy if I sit and dine with you this morning, Lass?"

"It would make me happy if you would go away," Talia replied.

"Stone of crows! Either we dine in peace, or I retreat to my study where I won't have to bear the sight of a pouting disposition." With piercing eyes, he looked into Poppy's downward cast. "Besides, I thought I ordered you to not let her out of the room for a week or longer."

Nobody responded.

Talia ignored him. He could sense her anger. His lips curved up in a lighthearted smile. "If you want, Lass, we'll walk around the manor. I think the fresh air would do us both good. Are you up for a lengthy walk?"

The idea of a walk thrilled her, but she didn't want him to think he had made her happy, so she tried to speak without emotion. "I'm certain I am fit to walk the length of your property all day long."

He smiled.

"Bertie, Poppy, I insist you join us for breakfast," Chatwin said.

"But sir..."

"I believe I insisted. *Now* sit!" Chatwin glanced over at Bertie and Poppy and gave them an appreciative smile.

"I can't believe how yummy this all tastes. Bacon, bangers, poached eggs, grilled tomatoes, and fried bread with the most sinfully delicious jams," Talia remarked, looking at Poppy. "After this breakfast, I shall need an excruciating exercise day. I hope, sir, you may keep up with me."

"No need to wonder. I know for certain, Lass, you may be unable to keep up with me."

Talia shot him a furtive glance. "Not today, but soon, sir,

would you be so kind as to honor me with a tour of your castle? Does it have enchantment like in the movie *Beauty and the Beast*? Any similarities?" she asked, her voice dripping with sarcasm.

"I hate to disappoint your vivid imagination, but you shall find no talking candelabra, teapot, cups, stool, or any such thing."

"Don't forget Cogsworth, the pendulum clock."

"Aye, but *that* you may find."

She smiled briefly, then covered her mouth with her hand so he wouldn't see it.

"Poppy, see that she dresses warmly and wears the proper footwear."

"I'm perfectly capable of choosing the right type of clothing and footwear, your Highness!"

"I have no doubt about that, princess. Good to go."

As Chatwin escorted Talia outside, he said, "Lass, there shall be no attempt to escape, or I shall confine you to your room once again. The electric fence has a remarkably high voltage. It could very well be fatal to the touch."

"You just couldn't drop the dictator speech for one minute, could you? Do you feel all mighty and powerful now, Mr. Oz?"

"I am regretting my gesture of a truce."

"Well, please, don't allow me to threaten any chance of making you seem human."

Just then, Poppy nudged Talia and gave her a scornful look.

Talia sighed and nodded. "Forgive me, sir, for my cheeky attitude. I'm grateful for any time you can spare and even more grateful for the freedom of roaming the premises."

His gaze softened, and he replied, "It is my pleasure. Bertie, Poppy, please see that a scrumptious lunch is prepared and set up in the courtyard. There may be a chill, but it is yet a lovely day. Do you approve, princess?" For once, his tone was cordial.

"Yes, sir, I would love that. Thank you, Poppy and Bertie."

Chatwin pointed out all the landscaping details as they walked while Talia identified the trees and flowers. He couldn't get over the adoring and charming ways she had with the critters and birds. He knew how much she loved animals, so he had stations all over the grounds with nectar and seeds, corn, and critter food. He watched as she dropped seeds and corn on the ground as she walked. The critters and birds came up, scampering around each other.

"Don't worry, little ones," she commented softly, "we have plenty for one and all." Her eyes were warm and welcoming. Chatwin watched her with soft eyes.

Giggling with sincere happiness, she felt alive and rejuvenated. They walked through the horse stalls. Horses neighed as Talia fed every horse, goat, cow, and deer. She laughed and carried on a cheerful conversation, proving herself quite intelligent in politics and important matters.

"'Tis refreshing to see a young woman so versed in politics. Most young women tend to have one thing on their minds —boys."

"Well, if not for my circumstances being cooped up in a grungy cabin room in the deep, deep forest, I may have reacted the same as normal girls. I didn't have that luxury. I would be beaten by those dreadful soap dodgers if I didn't keep up with my studies. The sultan wanted a beautiful and intelligent bride."

"I understand," he replied.

"Would you happen to know the outcome of Harry? Did he escape?"

"If you really care to know, I fear it is not a pleasant conversation to be had."

She looked at him curiously. "You know something. Something bad happened to him, didn't it?"

"I'm afraid so, Lass. When the authorities arrived at the cabin in the forest, they found Harry's body mutilated. I tend to believe it was the sultan's guards who killed him. The sultan and anyone from his country are never allowed in the UK again. For any reason. That's not all. Scotland Yard waited around for Percy and Norman to return. They are now in custody, in prison for life. It seems they were tricked into making that trip for nothing. The sultan planned to kidnap you and refrain from paying Percy what they agreed to pay. I guess that's poetic justice."

"But what crime were they arrested for since they know nothing about my abduction? Otherwise, they would want to speak to me. So, there was no way you could let them know how you abducted me."

"After a little digging around, I discovered a whole host of crimes they committed. There were already warrants out for their arrest."

"Oh, I see. So they don't know how you have abducted me, then?"

His shoulders rose up and down. His teeth grinded. "Would you prefer to return and be confined to the tower?"

"Yes, I would!" She strutted off, and he grabbed her arm. She swung her head around. "You will not bully me," she said, trying to release her arm from him. "It's better for me to return to the tower than let you die of a heart attack since you will collapse from trying to intimidate me into being your puppet. It won't happen!"

"I apologize. Will you forgive me? I haven't had much experience with people."

"No! You don't say."

His face grew red.

She straightened her hair and said, "I'll be nice if you will."

He nodded his head.

"Back to Harry and the rest of them. I guess it *is* poetic justice. I will not lie to you, but I realize I should be grateful to you for rescuing me from that horrible life. You *have* provided me with luxury and food fit for a queen—it's just not fit for me. I am simple in my desires. Bouquets of wildflowers and a boat ride down the River Coln is all the pomp and circumstance I need. However, I *am* having a divine day and wish not to fowl it up with negativity. So, if you don't mind, let's end our tour of the grounds in the gayest of moods."

"You have quite a good head on your shoulders, Lass, and yes, let us end this day on a good note. I promise you, there will be many more times like these to come."

They entered the side of the cliff where the sea roared in turmoil. As charming and beautiful as the landscape was, something was unsettling about it.

Chatwin glanced over and saw the fear in her eyes, but before he could console her, a huge wave crashed over the wall, soaking them both. The power of the wave was stronger than he had experienced to date. He glanced back at the sea defiantly, his hands forming into fists.

He grabbed Talia and pulled her away to safety. "That is the first time ever that the sea has managed its reach above the wall. I don't understand."

"I have this feeling deep inside," she said, holding her balled-up hand to her heart, "that the sea is alive and urging you to a duel. The anger in its roar is most intimidating."

"Aye, Lass, but make no mistake, my roar is louder and more powerful. It will not defeat me. Oh, how it has tried, but I always come out victorious as the waves bow down in surrender and defeat."

She was slightly concerned by his deranged statement, staring at his face in puzzlement. "Could we just go back and change our clothing for lunch, sir? I am so looking forward to eating in the courtyard."

"Of course, Princess. Of course."

They walked toward the castle as a powerful gust of wind swept by them, teasing and tempting Chatwin to come back to the sea and fight. He turned with a glare but kept walking. The chill caused Talia to hug herself. He noticed and wrapped his cape around her.

She glanced up at him with a smile to see what was under the cape. He was dressed in an expensive-looking sweater and casual trousers. Of course, he had his head turned so she couldn't see his face, which was always the case.

"Okay, Princess, please change into something warm and meet me in the courtyard."

Chapter Ten

When Talia walked outside to the courtyard, Chatwin sucked in a deep breath and tried to keep his face neutral. She looked angelic in a soft, white cashmere sweater and white linen slacks, with her satin skin and silky hair sparkling in the sunlight. She wore a small amount of makeup, which was flattering but unnecessary.

"This looks so divine. Is that a bouquet of wildflowers? They are so enchanting." She bent over and sniffed them, closing her eyes and smiling.

He couldn't take his eyes off of her.

A butterfly landed on the wildflowers, scavenging for a treasure chest full of sweet nectar. Talia watched it with delight. Then, after it had its fill, the butterfly fluttered onto Talia's finger. She slowly pulled her finger up near her face to study it.

Chatwin watched her in wonder.

She carefully maneuvered her finger toward a flower and blew a puff of breath, encouraging the butterfly to settle on the flower. Suddenly, a bunny hopped up to Talia. She giggled as she retrieved vegetables and fruit from the table. The rabbit nibbled from the palm of her hand.

Chatwin watched her with adoration.

Finally, Chatwin approached her, cleared his throat, and said, "Talia, I am sorry for all you have missed out on. If there is anything I can do to recreate some of those experiences, please ask, and it shall be done. Perhaps you would like to reenact a childhood moment or a special event."

Talia smiled at him. "Thank you. Unfortunately, there are things that money can't buy or that time can't heal. You can't replace a parents' love, the excitement of a school formal, or the feeling of being a silly teenager. I missed all these things, and thinking about it only makes me sad." She paused for a moment, lost in thought. "I'm sorry," she finally said.

"No, please don't apologize. I didn't mean to provoke feelings of melancholy".

Talia smiled as she stared at the landscape. "I was just thinking of memories. My mother used to decorate our house for Christmas. It was charming and giddy. The house made me feel like I was in a Christmas shop. Mother adored everything about Christmas. And at Halloween, she decorated with cute ghosts and bats. Every year, she tried a new way to scare me, for fun, of course." She sighed. "I guess I just miss holidays with my family," she interjected, staring up at the sky.

She was silent for a couple more minutes.

"Mother had the cutest scarecrows, many pumpkins, and big hay bales for the Harvest Festival. I suppose Christmas and Halloween are my favorite holidays."

He watched memories play through her mind, studying her expressions and how she used her hands for emphasis before he responded. "Aye, sounds like my mother. She also decorated for both holidays."

"Speaking of parents, could you let me know if my parents are well?"

"I will check into it and see what I can find out. I've been thinking about it, and I don't think it's fair for you to be cooped up in your quarters."

Talia covered her mouth with her hand to hide her smile.

Cooped up? Those quarters are humongous compared to what I've been accustomed to from my other abductors.

"So, if you promise not to try to escape," Chatwin continued, "I will allow you the freedom to roam the castle and the grounds. However, if you attempt to escape, I will have to confine you to your room, and I do not wish to make that happen. I do truly hope and care for your happiness. The entire estate will be accessible to you—except for one area. My chambers are off limits."

Talia pondered his words. *This is good news, but these lavish surroundings won't heal my heartbreak and loneliness. And freedom. It's still not freedom. These circumstances are better than your prior situation,* she chided herself. She looked up at Chatwin and smiled. "Thank you, Sir."

~

The next day, Chatwin took Talia for a horse ride. The day after that, he taught her to play badminton. Each passing day, Chatwin showered Talia with attention. She came to enjoy his company, but she grew curious about his appearance, as he always stayed disguised.

One day, she mustered up the courage to ask him about it. "You know, Sir, we have been spending much time together. Don't you think it is time you take off your mask? Even if you were deformed, even if you looked hideous, which I doubt, it would not matter to me."

He shot her a cautionary look. "That will never happen, and you should do well to never bring the subject up again."

"Well, don't count on it," she snapped defiantly and walked away quickly.

"Don't you dare walk away from me. That is an order!"

She stopped abruptly, turning slowly around with a sly smirk on her childlike face. "Or what?" Then, she proceeded to walk away faster.

"Or this!" He ran to her, grabbed her, and held her so tightly, she could not move.

She struggled against his strength, repulsed and enraged. Then, suddenly, a wave of magnetism flashed through her body, and for a second, she felt exhilarated in his arms. "Let go of me this instant," she yelled, trying to hide her sudden attraction.

Though Talia couldn't see Chatwin's face, his cheeks flushed as overwhelming desire consumed him. He wanted to touch her rose-colored lips with his, to feel her satin skin. *I haven't felt like this since*—he tore his thoughts away.

He let go of her and backed away. "I apologize, but I would appreciate it if you followed my instructions."

Talia straightened her hair and adjusted her sweater. "Fine. You've proven your brute strength. Are you happy? Now, if you don't mind, I would kindly like to resume my college studies. Or are you afraid I may prove to be more knowledgeable than you? I may not be able to show you up in strength, but perhaps I can surpass you in intelligence. I *can*, however, outrun you with my eyes closed."

"Is that so?" Chatwin asked with a smile. Still looking at Talia, he said, "Bertie, please set up a racing path to the front gate so the princess can show me her running skills. Make sure there are several guards at the gate. I fear the princess may be a sore loser and throw herself at the mercy of the high voltage."

"You're on. I will change clothes and meet you at the starting point," Talia said.

"Then be quick about it," he said with authority.

~

At the starting point, Bertie held up his hands and yelled, "On your marks, get set, go!" He swung the flag, and they took off like cheetahs.

Talia glanced furtively at Chatwin and realized they were

side by side. She sucked in a deep breath and ran faster, pulling away from Chatwin like a rocket.

Though Chatwin had been holding back, he sped forward now, catching up to her and speeding past her. Once again, Talia's competitiveness surged, and she pushed herself to go faster. She passed him, and then he passed her again. This continued until they approached the finish line.

Bertie watched carefully and announced, "Talia crossed the finish line first by a toe's length. She's the winner."

Chatwin smiled and shook her hand. "To the victor goes the spoils, My Lady. I can admit when I am wrong."

She smiled, nodded, and wondered if he let her win.

Poppy had lemonade waiting in the courtyard, so Talia and Chatwin plopped down in the chairs, both obviously exhausted.

Chatwin sipped lemonade and said, "This is so refreshing, Poppy. Thank you." He glanced at Talia and continued, "I did want to congratulate you on how well your college studies are going. Your grades are excellent."

"Thank you. I appreciate those kind words and you're staying informed of my advancements. I tend to believe that you are not much older than me. Don't worry. I would never ask you to divulge such personal information, even though, as history dictates, the woman is usually secretive of such matters."

"Aye. You *are* quite perceptive, but you are correct. I refuse to divulge personal information—even if you *did* win the race."

"That's what I thought you would say," she replied with a smirk.

The next week, Chatwin had gone away on business, so Talia chose a record to play in the phonograph to keep herself busy. As the music blared, she danced around like a teenybopper, singing and laughing. Hearing the loud music, Poppy and Bertie came in, and before long, the three of them were dancing.

Chatwin walked in unannounced and stood in the corner, watching in amusement. When Bertie noticed him, he froze. Then, Poppy and Talia noticed Chatwin, and they, too, stopped dancing.

"Please, don't let me stop you. You look as though you are having a jolly good time. Please, don't stop."

Talia slowly approached him as if she was pulled by an invisible string. She gently took his hand. Her touch shot electric waves through his veins, and he followed her as if in a trance.

Realizing she was asking him to dance, he pulled away from her and turned toward the door. "Come on. Dance with us. Please," she begged.

"No. I don't want to show you up," Chatwin said with a smile. "You go ahead and have fun."

"Pleease," Talia begged. "It'll be so much fun." She turned to Bertie. "Will you put on that Hootie and the Blowfish record?"

Bertie nodded and started a new album.

Chatwin huffed and said, "Okay, you asked for it." In an instant, Chatwin's body twisted and turned, performing old-style dances like *the Skate, the Frog, the Hitch Hike, and the Watusi.*

Talia fell to the floor, convulsing in laughter, kicking her feet in the air.

"I warned you fair and square," Chatwin said.

"So you did. I told you it would be fun."

"Aye, it was."

"Let's pick another record," Talia said.

Chatwin's jovial face turned serious, and he replied, "No. I can't. I need to get to my study. I have a conference call in—oh my goodness. In one minute. Good to go."

He grabbed his briefcase and left the room.

Chapter Eleven

T he temperatures dropped as fall approached, and
Chatwin hired a crew to decorate his estate for
Halloween, but he wanted to surprise Talia, so he asked
Bertie to keep her occupied while the crew worked their magic.
Bertie offered to take her horseback riding around the estate,
and she heartily agreed.

They galloped away from the castle on a crisp, cool October
afternoon. "Follow me," Bertie yelled. "I want to show you my
favorite spot on the estate."

When Bertie slowed his horse, Talia spotted a frothy creek
flowing through mossy rocks. Foam bubbled on the rocks and
bank, and fish wiggled through the narrow curves.

"Oh, it's beautiful, Bertie. Let's stop and water the horses,"
Talia suggested.

Bertie beamed as he dismounted his horse. "I thought you'd
like it."

On the creek bed, they sat in silence, listening to the
bubbling water, the croaking frogs, and the scampering sound of
critters in the vegetation surrounding the creek. The autumn
foliage was breathtaking.

Dipping her finger in the cool water, Talia realized something. As lonely as she was for her family and for the childhood she missed, she was falling in love with her new home. A look of melancholy overcame her face.

"Hey, why so sad, Lass?"

"It's the move—the move the Good Sir has informed us about. Don't you feel sadness about leaving this place? Why is he planning this move, anyway? Who would think I could feel sadness about leaving the place of my imprisonment, but sharing my time with you, Poppy, the staff, and even the old grouch himself, well... I don't know. Having the freedom to roam about and be with people I truly care about... well, it saddens me. Everything will change. You know it, Bertie."

Bertie lowered his head so she couldn't see his blurring eyes. Then he coughed to not expose his true feelings with his cracking voice. "I'm sure it will be different, but maybe we will love our new surroundings. We won't know until we arrive, but the good sir has been working day and night to make it splendid. You'll see. The location is a surprise for all of us."

She nodded her head.

Bertie received a text and remarked, "I do so hate to leave this spot. It is so peaceful and quiet—so beautiful, but I dare say it will be evening soon, so we need to head back to the stables."

"I'll race you."

"Okay," Bertie replied, grinning.

The galloping of horse hooves alerted the livestock crew of their arrival back at the manor. They helped Bertie and Talia off the horses and led the horses into the stall to care for them.

As Bertie walked Talia toward the castle, her eyes squinted as she tried to figure out what she was looking at. Bertie chuckled behind her back.

"What is that, Bertie?" she asked, pointing. "Come on. Hurry."

Chatwin watched from the window in his chambers as Talia ran around the grounds examining each ghost, goblin, and whatnot. As she pushed her way through the store-bought web filled with plastic spiders, she screamed like they were real, pulling pretend webs off her body.

Talia surveyed the hay bales and jack-o-lanterns in all shapes and sizes. She saw the headless horseman, bats, and unique decorations. When she turned the corner to the front door of the castle entrance, she spotted a ghost and wolf made of chicken wire among some trees. They looked so real, it gave her a fright.

When she opened the door to the manor, Talia giggled with delight as a recording made a creaking door noise. Inside the foyer, she walked right up to a life-size mirror, but when she glanced at her reflection, a monster stared back at her. She laughed out loud.

When Chatwin strolled into the foyer, Talia slammed into him for a hug.

"Ugh," he murmured, uncomfortable with the closeness.

It was always kept dark inside the castle, so Talia could barely make out his features, but shockingly, he wasn't wearing sunglasses, so she looked up into his eyes. She stared deeply into them and felt like she was falling into a deep cavern. A feeling of comfort enveloped her, and she lowered her head against his chest.

He gently pulled away and stood back, pleased by her reaction.

"My Sweet One, there is more. Check out your room."

She took off like a flash. Her tower was also decorated to the hilt. She giggled and investigated, her fingers touching everything. When she walked into the walk-in closet, her mouth dropped with fascination. A costume gown that favored Belle's on *Beauty and the Beast* was positioned across the countertop. An invitation informed her of a costume ball in two weeks for the household. She hugged the gown to her breasts and twirled around the room.

"Aw. Even *your* house is decorated, Tidbit. Look, you even have a costume. It is so precious."

~

The morning of the ball, Talia was forbidden to walk near the ballroom until the party. Chatwin stayed in his study all day, and Talia worked on her college studies and ate lunch in her room. She was so excited, she found it difficult to complete her assignments.

When it was time to dress, she took her time getting ready, fixing her makeup and hair to emulate Belle from *Beauty and the Beast*.

Bertie knocked on her door dressed as Lumiere and offered to escort Talia to the dinner table. They strolled into the dining room just as Mrs. Potts, aka Poppy, strolled in with a teapot and cups on a tray, and one cup, of course, favored Chip.

The cook walked out dressed as Cogsworth. *He even has the same tone of voice*, Talia thought with a giggle.

Suddenly, a silhouette of a huge beast shone on the wall. Talia placed a hand on her heart while an inward gasp rendered her motionless. She couldn't breathe. She was paralyzed as she stared at the shadow.

"Good evening," Chatwin said, stepping out from the shadow.

Talia stared at him, speechless. He was dressed in a costume as the beast. Goosebumps shivered over her body. Her heart fluttered. *Why am I feeling this way?* she thought.

"Good evening," she replied with a gulp.

Everyone ate an elegant meal and laughed the whole evening. Chatwin's mask covered his face with openings for the eyes, exposing his mouth and beard. Talia kept glancing at him, wishing he would remove the mask, shave his beard, and show her who he was. *Either he really is a beast, or he's hiding something important. Could he be a murderer?* With that thought, it felt like a cold ice cube ran down the back of her spine.

Just then, she looked up as Bertie snapped the camera, the

flash blinding her eyes. She blinked several times to regain her vision. "My goodness," she said, disoriented.

"It's time for dessert, Princess," Chatwin informed her.

Talia removed the stainless-steel cover before her and found a bowl of Kit Kat Chunky bars. She tore open a wrapper with enthusiasm. "My favorite candy bar, although, Crunchie Bar is fighting fiercely to be number one."

"Speaking of that," Charles added, and he removed another cover, revealing a bowl of Crunchie Bars. She felt them in her hands as they dropped to the table like she was handling gold coins.

Talia laughed and smiled at Chatwin, who rose from his chair and walked to Talia, extending his hand. She placed her hand in his white glove-covered hand and rose.

"The evening is still young," he said in a husky voice.

He led her to the ballroom and used both hands to open the doors forward. She couldn't stop smiling as he reclaimed her hand. As they waltzed around the room, she felt wonderful. She felt normal—a woman enjoying a splendid evening—not a prisoner.

She didn't want this night to end.

He didn't want this night to end, either.

After their dance, they strolled out to the terrace. The stars sparkled like diamonds in the sky, and Chatwin noticed how Talia's skin and hair sparkled right along with them.

"Talia, I've always wanted to ask. How is it that your skin and hair sparkle so? It's beyond enchanting but also *not* normal. You really appear as a princess right out of a fairy tale."

"Thank you, kind sir. I really don't know, but ever since I was old enough to explore on my own, heaven's light—something you witnessed yourself—shined a pathway to the most glorious, heavenly spot on Earth. This spot held a substance I call the dew of heaven. Just a touch to my lips gave me sparkling health, and it tasted sweet, like nectar, like nothing I've ever tasted. I contribute it to that. I feel as though the good Lord above enlightened me with a little piece of heaven. Why He chose me, I do not understand."

"That does make a whole lot of sense, if you think about it."

"If I were free—" she raised eyebrows in fun "—I could give Tidbit and his family a taste. At the time, I let my pet gerbil, Itsy, and my rabbit, Prince Chatwin, taste it, and they were healthy as can be."

"You named your rabbit Prince Chatwin? Why would you do that?" He gently pressed his hand to his stomach to ease the sudden nausea.

"There was this boy—silly me—that I would play with as a child. I always considered him dreamy, and he reminded me of a prince. He was kind and gentle, good and strong, even as a child. His intelligence was hard to match, and his wit was perfect. He was so perfect. I wonder what happened to him. You know, your eyes remind me of him."

"Is that so?" He changed the subject quickly, saying, "I have something for you. It goes along with our discussion."

"My curiosity is peaked." She fidgeted with anticipation.

He approached a round table and picked up a flat box wrapped in fabric. He handed it to her, and she looked carefully at the beautiful wrapping of fabric and the satin ribbon.

"I haven't had a gift in ages. I want to take a moment to unwrap it. Gifts have always been my one and only weakness. The anticipation of what is lying inside is exhilarating to me." She stared at the gift with soft, tearful eyes, then slowly untied the ribbon with shaky fingers, taking extra-long to open the lid. As she looked inside the box, her eyes grew big, and her smile matched her big eyes. "This is so perfect and so ironic at the same time. My name means 'Dew of Heaven'?"

"It most certainly does. The name is so befitting of you."

"Thank you. This means a lot to me."

"I know these living arrangements aren't exactly what you want, but you seem happy. Are you?"

"Aye. I didn't think it was possible, but I *am* happy. This will sound awfully familiar, but if I could only see my parents and Adelaide and Twiggly, just to know that they're well, that would mean the world to me. And even better, if I could let them know I am alive and well, I know it would ease their fretful dispositions. I can only imagine what they have been feeling."

"I'll see what I can find out. I promise." Chatwin's head drooped, and he suppressed a tear.

She reached out and touched his hand. "Are you okay?" she asked.

He pulled his hand from hers. "I fear, Princess, we need to call it a day. I have a busy day in the morrow. Are you good to go?"

"Aye, I am."

Disappointment shone on her face.

Chatwin, too, felt disappointment, but he walked away quickly to hide his emotions.

Chapter Twelve

This time of year, always changed Chatwin's mood like clockwork. The house staff conducted business with intensity, just waiting for the hurricane to hit—Hurricane Chatwin. He would be happy one moment and then mean as a rattlesnake the next.

The staff had warned Talia about the good sir's mood, so she tried to choose her words wisely that day. "Sir, I seem to notice a shaking rattle every time you enter a room. Perhaps a snake made its way into the castle and is following you around." With a coy smile, she held her hands to her mouth and pretended to make the music of a snake charmer, slowly swerving with her pretend flute playing.

"You are quite amusing, but this country does not have rattlesnakes. Vipera beras, yes. And you don't want to get on the bad side of that snake. Not to mention, it is cobras that snake charmers soothe—not rattlesnakes."

She smiled at him. "I know that. It was a joke. Snake charmers work with adder snakes, to be more precise," she corrected him as she walked away.

After her snake comment, Chatwin stayed in his quarters for days, which confused Talia immensely. Before the ball, he had been spending time with her every day, but now, she felt completely ignored. *What changed?* she thought. *Maybe I act too childish for him. Maybe he likes more sophisticated women.*

Suddenly, she was overcome with nausea. *Did I just imagine that he cared about me? And why do I care? He's holding me captive. And yet, I can't help my feelings. Despite my trepidation, I actually care for that beast, and I thought he cared for me. What an idiot I am.*

She fumed as she walked around the castle, noticing how immaculate and orderly it ran. It suddenly struck her how efficient, how copacetic the manor was handled—even when the good sir was holed up in his study. It was almost uncanny. She never heard him instruct anyone to pay the bills, clean the house, feed and care for the animals, or make repairs. It was like invisible forces managed everything.

Do I have to beg for a nibble of attention? she wondered as the servants continued their duties like any other day. *But why is his attention so important to me? It is crystal clear he rules over me like I am a caged animal, but at the ball, I felt like he was softening. He was fun to be around, even charming, in his beastly kind of way. What happened?*

~

In his study, Chatwin wrestled with his thoughts. At times, he truly hated Talia's presence—what it represented. He had felt himself being sucked in by her, and he knew he had to stop it. *No. I can't be around her at all. It could risk my whole plan, and my life would certainly become a state of doom if it didn't work out. Bertie doesn't even know all of it. Nobody does. I fear if I speak of it, I will retreat right back to the fragile mental person I became after my wife's death. It's final. I can't tell them the whole truth.*

"If I give in to her enchantment, it will ruin my revenge—my justified revenge. Actually, avenge is more of the appropriate term. Regardless, revenge, avenge, is justified," he consoled himself. "It is predestined. It was fate that I found her—almost as if God placed her right into my hands. Or is God setting a trap for me?"

He let out a roar of anguish and gut-wrenching pain.

The staff froze in fear. Seeing the household staff's faces, Talia ran to her room, locked the door, and cowered in a corner. *Maybe he is a beast, or maybe he is a murderer inflicted with guilt and shame.* As she wallowed in her trepidation, she smelled smoke. *What is that?* she wondered. "He's a dragon spewing fire from his evil nostrils. That's what I'm smelling."

Night after night, Chatwin paced in his chambers, unleashing bouts of anger and despair. His wretched roars produced unmistakable pain in his tone, and the roar echoed throughout the castle.

Hiding in the butler's room, Bertie shared a thought with Poppy. "Even the tetchy sea below seems intimidated and clammed up for a change."

She nodded in agreement. It hadn't been this quiet since she moved into the manor.

Talia hid in her quarters and listened fearfully. A groaning from outside her door caused her to lean against the wall and hold her breath. *If I open the door, will I die at his bloodthirsty hands? How much more of this can I take?* She clutched her head in her hands. *He is intimidating me! He enjoys the fear he creates amongst the staff—and in me.*

"I won't let you intimidate me," she yelled. "I refuse to live in such a hellish environment for your sheer pleasure. Do you want a virgin sacrifice? Is that what you want? Will that save the staff from your rage? Then, a virgin sacrifice is what you'll get."

And then it was quiet. She heard a door slam. She stomped out of her room and yelled for Poppy.

"I've had quite enough of his scare tactics. Is he mental, or what is his problem? How can you live with his ranting and raving? Has he ever hurt any of you?"

"No, Lass. I don't fear for my life, nor should you. It is rough on him this time of year. He never has been able to deal with it. We know enough to keep out of his way. It's just the way things are." She sighed.

"So it's okay for him to scare the bejeebies out of everyone? He is a beast, and this is unacceptable. I will not endure his despicable treatment of me or of any of you. This is it! I don't care what happens to me. I refuse to live this way, and so should you."

"I understand how you feel. I truly do, but I cannot explain any of it to you. I'm sorry." She placed a hand on Talia's shoulder.

"Yeah, yeah. You are afraid of him, too—obviously too afraid to stand up to him. Well, I'm not. I mean, it's not like I have anything to look forward to, nor do you, it seems. Haven't you ever wanted love and companionship?" Talia balled her fists up in anger.

"I understand what you're saying, but I lost my husband in war, and I have no children. My family have all passed away. You are like a daughter I never had, and these people are my family. I love them all—even the beast, as you call him." Tears glistened in Poppy's eyes.

"Oh, Poppy. I'm so sorry. I didn't mean to be so selfish. I love you, too, and Bertie, and even grouchy old Charles." She embraced Poppy, feeling ashamed of herself.

"Don't apologize, my dear," Poppy said. "I know it's a diffi-cult time. Bertie believes there is more to the story that turns our Good sir into such a beast. Bertie said the good sir started to tell him something once and then ran out of the room to his chambers. He didn't come out for a week. We were looking at family pictures at the time, and his countenance immediately switched from happy to—well, a beast, as you call him."

Talia pulled away and said, "If I'm being honest, I think I'm

85

just wishing for companionship, for love. I have been refused the opportunity to know what it feels like to be kissed, to feel flutters. Poppy, I must be psychotic or in desperate need of affection from a man because... well... for a while, I thought I had feelings for that—that monster. Anyway, please forgive me, Poppy, for sounding so inconsiderate to you. You mean a lot to me, and you always will."

Poppy brushed her hand down Talia's hair affectionately. "I know, Child. I understand more than you know. I don't know how we can help our Lordship through these tormenting times, but I have seen a change in him with you—a good change. It's just what this time of the year represents to him that is a curse from Satan himself, it seems. We don't know how to break the curse, but we do believe it will happen eventually. I believe that."

"Well, I hope so—for all your sakes."

Chapter Thirteen

Talia sat near the cliff daily, listening to the sea's mulish, uncompromising battle. Waves ferociously crashed against the cliffs, carving them away.

She stared absentmindedly out the window, dewy-eyed. Thoughts hit her tenderly. She stared at the rain falling and spoke in a mild, low tone, "Lord above, you feel my pain. I thought it may be rain falling, but it is obvious those are Your tears falling from heaven. You feel my sadness and cry with me. I do love You so, Lord."

She looked out beyond the cliffs, searching for her captor.

"I fear, good sir, the sea is not surrendering to your demands," she said aloud. "Quite the contrary—it is growing more obstinate. More aggressive."

She wondered if the castle could survive the sea's rage. Would it tumble into the ocean, and would they all tumble along with it?

Why haven't we moved off the premises yet? she wondered. *The castle is being packed, which is inconvenient to everyone, and it's bringing the rattlesnake out in Charles, more so than his normal rude behavior.*

"How could someone offer the hope of security and then

smash it to pieces and deliver outright fright instead. How? My existence is nothing but a mockery, with no apparent reason to live," she murmured sorrowfully.

Chatwin watched her sit at the edge of the cliff. "Enough! She doesn't deserve this. None of this is her fault. I must make amends like I do every year at this time," he yelled. She was one feather short of becoming an angel in his eyes. And conversation among staff confirmed his feelings.

$\sim$

Startled by the shadowy image on the cliff, Talia refused to look at him, keeping her eyes facing the sea.

"Might I have a word with you?" he asked.

"You must be imagining things. I am but an illusion. Invisible—or so it seems I have been so for weeks."

"I understand there is nothing I can say to make up for my actions, but I fear I have not been well. I beg your forgiveness. You certainly don't deserve any part of my monstrous ways. Do forgive me. I beg you."

"I will forgive you—with one exception. You take off your mask and confide in me what troubles you so."

"If that be your only exception, I fear I have to decline. Tis not a good idea to confess my troubles or my identity. It will only cause more suffering to you. I am so sorry."

She glanced at him then and looked tortured, as though he would cry as he turned to walk away.

"Sir, wait! I can see you live in torment. You are more of a prisoner than I am. I only wish to console you and be a friend. I will accept your apology as long as you spend time with me and apologize to your staff."

"I already have apologized and presented my staff with a substantial bunce and the opportunity to take some time off. Some of them have agreed to take time off, but some have nowhere to go and have declined that offer."

"I'm glad to hear that. I do have an urgent concern I would like to mention, but I don't want it to bring out the narky side of you."

"That is fair, and I won't get 'narky'. Please, continue."

"The waves below are growing stronger and out of control. I fear the cliff will tumble into the sea soon. Are we safe to be here?"

"I have called in a boffin just before I came to speak to you. So far, it seems we are fine, but my sources inform me that we will need to pay close attention regularly. I fear it is recompense for my evil deed in keeping you prisoner. Please don't worry. I shall not allow one person or animal on my estate to be injured by the rising, raging sea."

"Thank you, Sir. That does calm my nerves."

"Now then, could I offer you lunch in the courtyard?"

"That depends," she said with a whimsical look. "What are we having for lunch?"

"You certainly are a sassy lass," he sniggled. "I believe Charles told me he was making Toad in the Hole. Will that suffice?"

"It will suffice, but I will need exercise to lose the excessive amount of weight I will surely gain from it. I challenge you to a race after lunch, say forty-five minutes after."

"Aye, this time, you best be certain you will not exhibit poor sportsmanship after I beat you."

She laughed heartily, and he laughed with her.

Bertie and Poppy watched through the window, holding hands and dancing joyfully.

This time, Chatwin won the race by two feet.

"Did you let me win?" he asked earnestly.

"Don't be absurd. I was just too full from that divine lunch we ate. We will race again. Make no mistake about it."

"I have a surprise. If you promise you won't try to escape, I want to take you for a drive. We can go through a drive-thru for some burgers and shakes later. It will give you a chance to see the town of Anglesey. It is most lovely. Do you approve?"

She threw her arms around his neck and kissed him right on the lips. He felt dizzy, and he carefully pushed her away.

"I, good sir, shall get dressed and be down shortly," she said, skipping toward her tower.

"Bertie, Poppy, Charles, please inform all staff that you all have the evening off, except for my driver. I will be escorting Miss Talia around town, and we will go through a drive-thru for supper. I realize she needs to get out."

Chapter Fourteen

The next week, Chatwin took Talia out again. This time, they drove extensively around the countryside and through small towns. He had told her that he wanted to take her to a real restaurant this time, so he gave her a scarf to cover her hair, and she dressed in long sleeves and slacks. He also wore his usual disguise.

While they were out, Chatwin had a crew decorate the grounds for Christmas—and to surprise Talia for her birthday the next day. The entire staff had pitched in to make the surprise special. Even the cook agreed to bake a fairy cake.

At a coffee shop, Talia went to the loo while Chatwin remained at the table. When she didn't return after a few minutes, he glanced around nervously and twiddled his thumbs. "Is she taking too long?" he asked himself in a quiet voice.

Just then, Talia exited the restroom and noticed the exterior door just a few feet from her. For a minute, she stopped and thought, *I could run off. Should I? Do I really want to leave?* Her fingers fluttered nervously. *What's wrong with me?* she wondered as she walked back toward their table. Before she turned the corner, Chatwin walked up quickly, and they almost collided. Her hand went to her heart. "You gave me a fright."

He exhaled with a *whooo* sound. "I was just coming to check on you to make sure you were all right."

Her head tilted, and a sly smile spread across her face. "You thought I was going to try and escape."

"Not at all," he lied as he escorted her back to the table.

When they returned home, Talia spotted two large fir trees covered with multi-colored lights.

"What is going on? Look, Sir. Just look! The whole castle is lit up. What must it look like inside?"

"I can only imagine it is spectacular inside as well. I hope you like it."

"Like it? I love it. Is this all for me?"

"Aye. It is."

"It makes me feel so happy, just like when I was a small child. Thank you. So much!"

"It is my pleasure. Before you came, I hadn't decorated the house for many years. Having you here and seeing your delight is refreshing. It even brings joy to my heart. So, in turn, I thank you."

Chatwin grew quiet as he thought about the upcoming Christmas holidays. *I pray I don't turn into a beast when it gets close to Christmas. It will tear her apart. But I can't seem to control the rage. It just happens out of nowhere. Poor lass. And now, spending time with her is addictive. I feel like I can't be away from her, like I need to be with her—I want to be with her. I do love being with her. Oh, me, oh my.*

"Are you okay, sir? You seem lost in thought."

"I'm just fine. Really, I am. Oh, you can't go into the dining room until we tell you it is okay. Promise?"

She studied his face with curiosity. "As you wish."

"Also, Charles, Bertie, and Poppy have something splendid awaiting us."

She took his hand as they exited the car and said, "Come with me. Let's look around the castle at the decorations. Come on. Move it, Sir."

He allowed her to pull him around the castle, hand in hand. Bertie and Poppy watched out the window, crossing their fingers in glee.

"Oh, Sir, this is beyond incredible. You even have a manger scene. Momma and Poppa have one they put out every year. Okay, now, let's go see the inside. The reindeer and sled are elegant. The Christmas mice are adorable. Let's get inside." She pulled him, coaxing him to walk faster.

As they walked in the door, mugs of hot cocoa and a plate of frosted sugar cookies awaited them.

"This is splendid," Talia cooed.

They both grabbed a cookie and drank hot cocoa while looking at the room. Next, Talia hugged Bertie and Poppy, and even grouchy Charles. She skipped around room to room and then ran to the tower. In her quarters, she held her hands over her mouth like she was keeping herself from screaming, her eyes as big as saucers.

"I can't believe it. Tidbit, just look at your house. It's as beautiful as mine."

She heard Christmas music. Paul McCartney was singing "Wonderful Christmastime," and shortly after that, the rock band Wizzard played *I Wish it could be Christmas Everyday*. She twirled to the music and stopped as Chatwin strolled into her room.

"Everything is sensational. Everything. I don't know how to thank you properly." She slammed into him and hugged him tightly.

"Good to go. Now, I fear I must attend to business. I shall see you in the morning. Good evening, Lass."

"Good evening, good sir." Her eyes twinkled as she watched him walk away.

Just then, Poppy strolled into her room with a package. "Your package arrived."

"Thank you, Poppy. Oh, Poppy, I had such a wonderful time tonight. I am so happy. And, if you think about it, I am a prisoner. It doesn't make sense to be happy." Then she told Poppy everything they did that evening. She fell asleep that night with butterflies in her stomach and a smile on her face.

The next morning, she wandered into the kitchen with a wide-mouth yawn and was served her favorite breakfast: black pudding, baked beans, bubble and squeak, fried bread, toast, marmalade, grilled tomatoes, and grilled pears, and, of course, hot tea.

"Oh, my, you are trying to make me fat, but I can't refuse this. I have to eat everything. Everything! How could you?" she said with a whimsical smile.

Charles smiled.

"Good day, Lass. I presume this breakfast is to your liking?" Chatwin asked gleefully.

"You presume right. I will go for a run shortly after. Thank you, sir, for letting me buy an outfit, but after this breakfast, I don't know if it will fit me."

"I would accompany you, but I must depart shortly for a business meeting in town. I shall return before supper."

"I'm glad you'll be back. Honestly, I would be terribly upset if I didn't get to spend time with you." Feeling her cheeks blush, she looked down.

"Well...uh..." Chatwin stammered. "Stay out of the dining room, Lass. Charles, Bertie, Poppy, I insist you join us for breakfast. Un-un. Join us, please."

After they all had their fill, Chatwin patted his stomach and leaned back in his chair. "I fear I may be too full to move. Charles, excellent brekkie, as is all the cooking you do. Bertie and Poppy, I don't know what I would ever do without you."

"Aye, good sir. We are more than grateful to work for you. You be near and dear to our heart," Bertie replied.

Talia smiled almost tearfully.

Tears formed in Chatwin's eyes, and he quickly blinked them away. "Well, I must be off," he said, standing abruptly.

Talia stared out the window as he walked to the car. When

he reached his driver, he said something and patted him on the back. The driver looked emotional, and Talia saw him mouth 'thank you' to the good sir. At that second, Chatwin glanced at the window and waved at Talia. She waved back, feeling like she would be lifted in the air by all the butterflies inside her.

～

Poppy informed Talia that she needed to dress nicely for supper in the dining room that night. "Dinner will be served at 7:00 o'clock on the dot. Don't be late, Miss."

"I won't be late."

Everyone was in a cheery mood that day—even Charles. *Must be the Christmas decorations,* Talia thought. *Christmas makes everyone happy.*

At 7:00 p.m., she cautiously walked toward the dining room, confused as to why it was so quiet. *You could hear a pin drop,* she thought. *Where is everyone? And why is it so dark in here?* A flash of fear shimmied through her body.

When she took a tentative step into the dining room, the lights flashed on, and she heard a roaring yell. "Happy Birthday!"

She looked around and saw all the staff wearing party hats. Confetti rained down on her, and she heard blares of party horns.

She was so surprised and overwhelmed, she didn't notice Chatwin standing in the corner, but he certainly noticed her. *What an outfit,* he thought as he studied her snug-fitting, short-sleeved dress. It was short and black with a low-cut back.

She was laughing and carrying on a conversation, unaware of his gaze. Her white-blonde hair hung in front of her in a low ponytail. *She's gorgeous, sensual, and feminine. And with the way her hair and skin sparkle, she really is a sight to behold.*

Staring at her, Chatwin was instantly transported to his childhood. He saw them as children laughing and wrestling on the ground, rolling back and forth in the dirt.

"This is so dench," Talia spoke, pulling Chatwin out of his revelry. "How did you know it was my birthday? You have no idea how much this means to me. The cake... oh, the cake is a piece of art. Thank you so much."

Chatwin watched as she went around the table, hugging and kissing his staff members on their cheeks. Before long, she noticed him standing in the corner. She smiled, walked toward him, and embraced him in a long hug. When she pulled back, she kissed him on his cheek slowly and deliberately.

"You..." He paused, unable to piece together a thought. He cleared his throat and tried again. "You like?" he managed to say.

"Not at all." She suppressed a laugh. "I love."

His body released its tension, and a slight sigh escaped his lips. "Um... well, I'm happy that you're happy. Now, let's enjoy the party," he said.

They spent the evening devouring a supper fit for a queen. The cake tasted so sinfully delicious, she was embarrassed about how much she ate. After dinner, the staff presented her with gifts, and she made a big fuss over all the presents, kissing the staff's cheeks in gratitude.

"Talia, if you don't mind, I have a special gift for you," Chatwin told her. "At least I hope it will be for you in your room. Would you be okay if I accompany you while you open it?"

"I would be delighted for you to accompany me."

She grabbed his hand and pulled him along to her room, stopping and rubbing her hand gently over all the decorations as they walked.

"You know, if I were your father, I would never let you out of the house wearing that outfit."

"Well, it's a good thing you're not my father." She smiled slyly at him. "Besides, I doubt you're old enough to be my father. I have a feeling that you're not much older than me, though I can't tell for sure because you always wear that silly disguise."

"No comment," he said with a grin as they entered her quarters.

She spotted a beautifully wrapped gift on the bed. She went, sat down, and patted the bed. "Come. Sit beside me," she remarked.

He gulped with trepidation but obeyed.

She unwrapped the gift with the excitement of a child. "The wrapping is beautiful. Now, let's see what's inside." She carefully tore the paper. "Oh. Ohhh," she mouthed emotionally, and suddenly, she was crying.

Chatwin couldn't tell if it made her upset or if she was happy.

Talia wiped away her tears and slowly took his hand. "This means the world to me. I can see I've been wrong about you. You are no beast. You are a good man."

"Don't get carried away with your kind words. After all, you are still my prisoner."

"A happy prisoner at that."

"My father looks so thin," she said as she rubbed his face in the framed photograph. "My mum's smile looks forced. Oh, how my disappearance must be mortifying to them. I do hope that they are well." Still holding his hand, she whispered, "I don't know how you got this picture, but I thank you from the bottom of my heart."

"You're welcome," he said, pulling his hand away tersely. He stood.

Before he could escape, she grabbed his arms and pulled herself to a standing position. Then, she kissed his lips. The butterflies in her stomach fluttered, and she pulled back. "I'm sorry, Sir. I'm just so thankful for your gift…"

Chatwin's stomach knotted up, and against his better judgment, he grabbed her face gently, staring into her eyes. Then he ran his fingers through her hair and trailed kisses from her cheek down to her mouth. He slowly parted her lips with his tongue. She accepted with desire, her body shuttering. His hands lingered on her neck, and his breathing had become heavy and labored.

Tingles of pleasure and joy vibrated through Talia's body, and she moaned slightly.

Being lost in the moment, they didn't hear Poppy enter the room. Her hand went to her mouth. "Excuse me, Sir," Poppy commented, embarrassed. Her face blushed.

He jumped back from Talia. "Forgive me, Lass," he said, bolting out of her room.

"Miss, I am so sorry for intruding," Polly said.

"It's okay. It's probably best that you did. I don't know what may have happened between us, but I do know what would *not* happen. I fully intend to be a virgin upon my wedding day. Is that a silly notion?"

"Not at all. It is noble."

"Look, Poppy. A picture of my parents. It is so thoughtful. How did he get it?"

"I don't know, but I do know he wanted your birthday to be special. Miss, he cares deeply for you, but I think he is scared to acknowledge it."

"I fear I, too, am scared to acknowledge my feelings for him."

"Would you like me to pour you a bath?" Polly asked.

"No, thank you. I'm going to play with my mice for a while."

"Good evening, miss."

"Good evening, Poppy."

Before turning into bed, Poppy decided to check in on Talia. With her arms wrapped around her knees and her head resting on her arms, Talia rocked slowly.

"Follow your heart, even if love takes you to the stars in the heavens or down into the depths of the sea. Reach high, my dear," Poppy commented.

Talia rose and threw her arms around Poppy, hugging her tightly. "I will, sweet Poppy. I will."

~

Chatwin tossed and turned that evening, thinking about his foolishness with Talia. But he couldn't stop thinking about that kiss and the electrifying sensation that ran through his body. It was far more than a physical reaction.

"Her kiss tasted like honeysuckle nectar. It was tantalizing, fulfilling. It was pure enrapture. That angelic voice, the flocculent feel of her skin, and the organic fragrance of her hair, like fresh air mingled with wildflowers—it was all so enticing. She is callow and sensual, good and kind. Plus, she is quite intelligent. Not to mention her stubborn and persistent mannerisms. She's perfect, and nobody is perfect," he said.

His thought lingered on. *She is dangerous, and her touch is toxic,* he thought. *I must stay away from her for a while, or I shall fail. But she doesn't deserve any of this. It is not her fault, so why am I so determined to take it out on this angel?*

"It's a trap, isn't it, Lord? I have to pull it together because my plan is righteous indignation. A life for a life, and yet her life shall remain alive."

~

Talia couldn't sleep either. She twirled around the room, opening and closing her eyes, heart going pitter-patter. She thought about the kiss—his earthy, woodsy flavor was so invigorating.

"I could feel his desire, Tidbit," she said, lying on the bed facing him on her stomach. "The fire burning inside of me was petrifying. I didn't want it to stop. I never imagined all the emotions that a kiss could conjure up after the repulsive kiss that Harry forced on me." Her nose crinkled at the thought. Her body shuddered.

"But he ran out of here so fast. Now, he'll regret what

happened and hide from me. I just know it. I don't want it to end. Ever."

Then she turned over on her back and looked heavenward. "I mean, doesn't your Word, Lord, say that 'all things work together for good to them that love the Lord'? I love You, Lord, so what was meant for bad is turning into something good. Please, don't let regret take hold of him. It's too late for me, for I have fallen in love—and not the silly schoolgirl kind of crush, but something more meaningful. Lasting. Don't fail me, Lord. I beg You that I may be in good standing with You.

Chapter Fifteen

"Your Lordship, Talia confided in me, and she is most perplexed. Would you allow me to speak openly with you?"

Chatwin rolled his eyes, stretched his legs in front of him, and crossed his arms. Chatwin shot Bertie a malevolent look.

"I have no intentions of being so bold as to interfere in your personal affairs, and you can attest to such in reviewing my service to you throughout the years. However, sweet Talia is fearful you may cease all contact with her because of the moment you two shared. She is most upset, crying, and unable to eat or sleep. Please don't hurt the young lass. She is so very important to all of us. My, how she has brought light into darkness. It's as though the good Lord up above dropped her into our care and enriched all our lives. Why, even her appearance takes on a heavenly glow."

"And just how did you find out about the moment we shared? Poppy was instructed not to mention it to anyone. I will deal with her betrayal." Chatwin pushed himself up in the chair, his hands balled into fists.

"No, please, sir. She didn't know what to do about Talia and needed to confront the matter to someone. She is terribly frightened of you, sir. Please, I beg you to not scorn or excuse her from service."

He hung his head. "She's frightened of me? Am I that horrible? Bollocks! Why do you all stay then?"

"Because we all know how special you are, sir, regardless of your mood swings."

"Please understand, dear Bertie, that sometimes I don't even recognize my actions.

I shall apologize to Poppy, but please do not mention what happened with Talia to anyone else. It was one of my weak moments, and it shall not happen again."

"Sir, I don't want to anger you, and I am not prepared for a bollocking, but..."

"Then that's a horrible way to start." Chatwin sat down, relaxing against the back of the chair, and crossed his arms again.

"It's just that you and Talia seem to have a connection, and she seems to make you happy. Don't you think it is time to release her?"

Chatwin heaved a sigh but paced his answer, so he didn't explode. "I believe I have made it clear the reason for this abduction. An injustice has been done simply because of the politics behind the crime. It is unfair, and I will not change my mind until he has paid for his sin.

"That was a weak moment for both of us, but my head is back in the game. I will not lead her into a false hope of a relationship that will go nowhere. I will not! Never bring this up to me again. She is being well taken care of and even happy. That should suffice. Now, do I make myself clear?"

"As clear as the air I breathe, your Lordship, but I must say that it's sad how you have grown so much older than your actual age. I fear you have missed out on youthful days by taking over such exhausting duties, including the household of your late father, a good, good man. May he rest in peace. Sir, please allow time for youthfulness before you grow too old to enjoy it and grow bitter because of all you gave up."

"Certain circumstances require growing up and not being influenced by silly, youthful notions. It's not my fault."

"I beg to differ, your Lordship. Have a good evening."

After Bertie left, Chatwin spoke aloud to himself. "He's right. I can't punish her for being weak. Could she be an angel right out of heaven, sent to bring light into our lives? Could that be what causes that glitter? I wonder."

He got up, stretched, threw on his hoodie and sunglasses, and then roamed the castle looking for Talia.

"Poppy, Bertie, where are you?" Chatwin roared.

"In here, your Lordship." Poppy walked out, seeming disinterested.

"Are you okay? You seem a little down."

"I'm fine, your Lordship. I think I'm coming down with a cold. That's all."

"I want you to go lie down and not worry about any duties until you are a hundred percent. If you should feel worse as time passes, please alert me immediately. That is an order, by the way." Anytime he let down his guard and showed affection to his staff, he wrestled with the thought of damage to his heart, should something tragic happen to any of them. Could his heart take that ever again? He hadn't recovered from past tragedies.

"Yes, your Lordship. As you wish." She was walking toward the door when Chatwin remembered why he called for her in the first place.

"Oh! Poppy, before you go, where might Miss Talia be?"

"She's been outside for quite a while. Bertie went out about twenty minutes ago to find her."

"Thanks, Poppy." Chatwin rushed outside, calling her name and searching with determination.

He yelled her name louder and louder as he ran. He ran for an hour until he finally found her at the creek.

"Talia, are you okay? Why are you crying?"

She took some uneven breaths and whispered, "FlipFlop."

His face wrinkled in confusion, and his head shook three times. "You're upset about your flip-flops?"

Her frown curved up into a gentle smile. "No, silly. *This* Flip-Flop." She carefully raised a fluffy rabbit from her lap. "He's sick. Something's wrong. I visit the bunnies almost every day and bring them fruit and veggies, but he won't eat. I call him Flipflops because his paws look like flipflops." She lifted his paws for Chatwin to examine. "Oh, and this is TippyToes. She has black tips on each toe." She lifted another rabbit up for him to examine. "I'm so worried."

"You do fret over your critters."

Bertie strolled up on a horse. "Ah, Bertie, I'm glad you're here," Chatwin said. "We must get Flopflip and Toetips—or whatever their names are— to the veterinary immediately. Please be quick about it." He handed the rabbits to Bertie.

"Absolutely, Sir," Bertie said, galloping off with the bunnies.

"Now, let me help you up," Chatwin said. He grabbed her hand and pulled her up. "They will be given the best care. Please don't worry."

"I can't help it. My animals mean the world to me. You should be aware of that by now."

"Aye, I am. Let's get you back to the house so you can have some hot chocolate."

"That's a good idea, and it's a castle, not a house," she said with a smile.

"Whatever you say."

"You'd be good to remember that remark." She looked at him mischievously with her lips slightly puckered. "How did you find me?"

"I looked for anything that sparkled."

"The stars sparkle. Did you look for me up in the sky?" she asked as they walked back to the castle.

"Now that you mention it, yes. I've come to believe you are an angel of God. There is no other rational reason for your magnificent appearance." Talia blushed. "By the way, Poppy isn't feeling well, so I told her to go lie down until she feels better. If you should need anything, I'm sure Bertie or Charles may help you."

"Or you?"

"I have business to tend to, as you well know."

"Well, maybe my well-being should be as important to you as it is to Bertie, Charles, and Poppy."

"Someone has to handle the income and business dealings."

"I'm certain you have many assistants outside of these walls who attend to your business at any time at your beck and call. Am I right?"

"You are different than most young women your age. You have a good head on your shoulders, or someone in my service is a big blabbermouth."

"Don't be absurd. Your staff refuses to tell me anything about you, and it makes me darn mad. Since I haven't had the opportunity to act my age, this is the result."

"Have you decided what direction in life you desire to study? I would think it should have something to do with animals or Biblical theology."

"You would think, but I want it all. I want to help animals, help people, and learn how to study the Bible. Plus, I'd like to be a botanist, a prominent political figure, an archeologist, a psychologist, a forensic specialist, a historian, and a spy. Plus, I want to sing, work with children, and much, much more. I can't make up my mind. But what does it matter anyway? I am a prisoner and won't have a chance at a career."

"Life has a way of surprising us. Don't give up hope," he said as they approached the castle.

She paused, looking up at him. "How long are you going to let that scruffy beard grow? You don't need that hoodie to cover your face anymore," she said, touching his beard.

He stepped back from her abruptly. "Tis not your concern. Now get in the house."

"Castle."

"Fine. Get in my castle."

"Is that an arrogant tone coming out of your mouth?"

"Why, yes, it is." He cracked a smile.

"Hey, you wouldn't want to watch *A Child's Christmas in Wales* with me, would you?" Talia asked.

"I would. I never miss that movie during the holiday."

Her pearly, white teeth gleamed with affection. She glanced around the room at the Christmas decorations and let out a happy sigh.

"With Poppy resting, I should make us some popcorn, then," Chatwin uttered.

"Do you think you can handle such a task on your own?"

"You cut me to the quick, Lass. Anyone can throw a pack into the microwave. Even me."

"Will miracles never cease?"

"You are just full of wit this evening. I'll be back in a jiffy."

"Cheerio."

～

After the movie, Talia and Chatwin were still munching on popcorn, talking about their favorite Christmas movies, when Bertie strolled into the family room.

"Oh, Bertie. How is FlipFlop? Is he okay?" Talia asked.

Bertie smiled. "No! *She* is giving birth and in good hands."

"What?" Talia exclaimed. "FlipFlop is a she?"

"Yes, and TippyToes is a 'he.' I will pick them up on the morrow, and before you ask, they are all scheduled for preventative birth control, good sir."

"You know me well. Thanks," Chatwin replied.

"What's all the commotion about?" Poppy asked, holding onto the back of the couch to keep herself from falling.

"Hello, my dear. I brought you some chicken soup," Bertie responded.

"And you look like you need to get back in that bed. Do you need help?" Chatwin asked, pushing himself up from the chair.

"No, sir. I'll make it just fine." Poppy took one step and fell flat on her face.

"Poppy! Sir, help her," Talia screamed. She ran to Poppy's side and kneeled on the floor beside her. She felt Poppy's forehead. "She's really hot."

"Bertie, handle things while I take Miss Poppy to the emergency room," Chatwin announced. "Get me a blanket and my wallet—quickly, please."

Talia sat next to Poppy with tears streaming down her face. "I love you, Poppy.

Come back home quickly."

Chatwin covered Poppy with a blanket and picked her up in his arms. It looked easy for him, even though Poppy was on the plump side. "I shall stay with her until I know for certain she will be okay."

Talia noticed that his voice cracked as if he was about to cry. *He really cares about her. I'm so touched by his devotion.* "I shall pray for her, good sir."

"Aye, see that you do. If anyone can get the Lord's attention, it would be you. Pray with fervency, Lass."

"You can count on me."

The helicopter was up within minutes.

The phone rang, and Bertie answered it. "Oh, no, sir. How is she now? Please keep us posted. She means a lot...a lot to me—to all of us, sir."

"Bertie, what did he say?"

"It seems Poppy has pneumonia. Do not give up hope and keep praying. The doctor feels we may have caught it in time."

"And what about the beast—I mean his Lordship. How is he taking it?"

"Not well. He was trying to be his usual tough and unaffected self, but I could hear the worry in his voice. Of course, I may never speak of such to him— nor should you."

"I totally understand. I'm going to resign for the evening and be in prayer."

"Good night, Talia," Bertie said.

Before exiting the room, Talia turned around and said, "You're in love with her, aren't you?"

"I do love her."

Talia smiled and approached him. "Bertie, I promise not to try and escape if you want to go visit her in the hospital. I promise." She patted his hand.

"I cannot. It would make him furious to leave you, and you have seen how bad it can get."

"Tell me about it. Good evening, then." She bent over and kissed Bertie's cheek.

"Good evening, sweet Talia."

~

The helicopter landed at 5:00 a.m. Chatwin, totally exhausted, walked slowly toward the manor. Before he opened the front door, Bertie and Talia ran out.

"Good sir, is Poppy fair?"

"Is she?" Talia asked impatiently, not allowing him to respond to Bertie.

"She is out of danger, but she will be in the hospital for at least five days. She is doing well, though."

"You look bad—so tired, an emotional wreck, if I may be so blunt," Talia said.

"It has been a long evening. I need to get some sleep. Bertie, please cancel all appointments tomorrow—well, today, actually. If you are too tired, call my assistant—yes. You take the day off. Please call her, and she can take care of it."

"Yes, good sir."

Her? Talia thought. *The person he spends the most time with is a her?*

~

At noon, Talia and the rest of the staff entered the kitchen after some much-needed rest. Charles had made them breakfast, and they all ate together. Even Charles sat down to eat.

When the phone rang, Bertie literally ran for it. "Hello. Good day, Miss Poopy."

He was so nervous, he didn't realize he mispronounced her name. Everyone at the table lowered their heads and chuckled.

"It's good to hear your voice. Splendid. I shall inform everyone of the great news. Take care of yourself."

"How is Miss Poopy?" Chatwin said, laughing as he entered the kitchen.

Bertie suppressed his embarrassment and, in his usual professional manner, said, "She is splendid, good sir."

Talia turned her head to hide her smile from Bertie.

"I expect you will go visit her?" Chatwin asked Bertie.

"Yes, good sir. If you wouldn't mind."

"I should feel nothing but shame if you didn't. Get out of here, and don't worry about returning anytime soon. By the way, I had my assistant fill Poppy's room with flowers. You may want to take a bee repellant. As many flowers as the room can hold, I'm sure the floral scent has alerted the bee kingdom."

Talia giggled at the wit of his words. The more she got to know him, the more she saw how intelligent and fun he truly was—especially with words. More impressive, though, was his heart-wrenching love and devotion for his help—and how he tried his darndest to hide it. And it wasn't just his help. What type of beast would consider the well-being of the rabbits in an emergency and get the help immediately? If he was such a good man, why did he persist in keeping her a prisoner, and why did he abduct her in the first place? Nothing made sense.

～

Four days later, Talia approached Chatwin with pleading eyes, and her hands steepled as if in prayer. "Christmas is in two weeks. Any possible chance we could drive around and look at all the wonderful decorations? Please, I beg you."

"I assume reading minds is one of your angelic traits? I planned on spending the day and evening doing just that, but you would, however, need to be in disguise, I'm sorry to say. Even with a disguise, I'm still a bit worried, though. I plan to walk you through some shops and such."

She glared at him.

"I'm sorry. When I look at you, I often feel like a spell has been placed on me."

"Don't be absurd. What, you think I'm a witch?" Her fists rested against her hips.

"No. *Are* you?"

"You may leave and never come back."

"How can I do that? I happen to live here." He shrugged his shoulders, raising his hands in surrender. "I'm sorry, but there's something hypnotizing about you. Your skin is snow white. You would stick out like a sore thumb even among residents of Antarctica because of that silky, sparkling color that radiates from your skin. Lying in fresh-fallen snow, you would blend in, the way it sparkles like diamonds. And your hair is silky, almost white, sparkling like the stars in the midnight sky. Even your majestic midnight blue eyes sparkle. I'm sorry, but I can't help but assume there is something mystical about you."

"Well, I am not a witch, sir, if that is what you are implying. I hope I haven't disappointed you."

Chatwin looked at her face. *The old line, if looks could kill, is unfortunately true.*

"Well, if you *are* a witch, you're definitely a good witch. There is nothing disappointing about you." He smiled a boyish grin that caused flutters in her heart. Then, he came to his senses and gained his composure. The smile on his face switched to an icy cold hardness.

You're not disappointing to look at either, even though your mood changes like Jekyll and Hyde. Talk about Prince Charming—straggly hair, beard and all. I know you are handsome under all that rubbish, though.

"Anyway, forgive me for suggesting you're a witch," Chatwin said. "I never intended to imply such a thing. It's just... it's just how your hair and skin sparkle... and the charm you have over people... it makes me curious. I mean, Charles? I have never met anyone who could lure him into a gleeful mood until you."

"As flattering as you have attempted to be, your statement aches with insult. If I were a witch, as you *did* suggest, don't you think I would have cast a spell over you and conquered your castle for my own—not to mention gaining my freedom?"

"I fear you have done just that. You roam the castle and grounds as if it's your own. And if you continue to be on the good list, maybe St. Nick will give you all your wishes."

"*All* my wishes?"

"You have heard the saying, 'Be careful what you wish for'."

"Aye, I have," she replied, secretly wishing for more alone time with him.

Chapter Sixteen

T he Christmas lights, the cheerful decorations, and the smells of Christmas delighted Talia. The next couple weeks, she spent time with Chatwin, driving around looking at decorations and eating at restaurants and pastry shops. They drank coffee and hot cocoa from a café and went shopping. It was a dream come true.

She couldn't quit smiling, and she couldn't quit hoping that even better days lie ahead. One day, as they walked through a shop, she grabbed his hand and pulled him toward the Christmas section. For once, he didn't pull away from her. That day, they bought more Christmas decorations, and she couldn't help herself from buying tree ornaments of the *Beauty and the Beast* movie.

"So, I guess I'm the beast? Do I really look that hideous?" Chatwin asked as they left the shop. "And if I might add, you look nothing like Belle."

"Are you implying that *I* am hideous? If you are, sir, from what I can see, *you* are the hideous one. Obviously, that's what you're trying to hide behind that straggly beard and hair disguise."

"Oh, really? I think that statement deserves this!" He

quickly formed a snowball and hit her with it.

She dropped her bags. "Two can play at this game." They hit each other over ten times before falling to the ground, laughing heartily.

"Well, now that you have spent all my money, I think we should head home. Did you enjoy yourself?"

"So much. Thank you. I found some really great gifts for the staff. What about you?

Did you remember to buy them something?" she asked with excitement.

"I give them all a hefty bunce at Christmas."

"Is that it? Nothing personal?"

"You would think a hefty bunce is quite personal, would you not?"

"It *is* great, but you should consider giving it to them with something personal from you. It doesn't have to be expensive. It could be something as simple as a picture or a food or pastry they adore. Something from the heart."

"Hmm. I see your point." His index finger tapped his lip as he looked up in thought.

"I may need your assistance picking out the perfect gift to accompany the bunce."

She rubbed her hands together, and her smile gleamed. "I shall be more than happy to help. Let me dig around and see what I can find out, and I'll do it quickly since we only have two weeks 'til Christmas."

"Perfect." He dialed his driver's cellphone number.

On the way home, Chatwin sat deep in thought. *I love spending time with her. I always did. As a child, I always looked forward to our play dates. Is it possible to fall in love twice in a lifetime? No, I can't let that happen. Being in love with Talia will change the outcome, and he deserves one that ruins his life. But does she deserve to pay with her life*

for someone else's dastardly deed? He rubbed his temple back and forth with his fingers.

"Is everything okay?" Talia asked.

He replied coolly, "Yes, it is."

"I don't mean to be forward and upset you, but your mood swings go from hot to cold instantly."

"You are quite perceptive. For some odd reason, a bad memory popped up, but I don't want to end this enjoyable evening with thoughts that could ruin it. I apologize."

"Apology accepted. Jonesy, would you mind playing Christmas songs?"

"I thought you'd never ask," he replied.

Chatwin feared hearing one particular song. If he heard it, he knew it would send him over the edge. His hand gripped the door handle.

"The store was pretty busy today, but the decorations were so beautiful, and I really like that Christmas tree at the front of that last shop we were in, and I loved the colored lights on it..." he babbled.

"My, you have turned into a Chatty Cathy," she remarked in bewilderment.

"I'm sorry. I just felt like talking. Is that so bad? I mean, you always get angry if I ignore you. Make up your mind, would you please?"

She uncrossed her legs and sat up straight, looking at him defiantly. "Don't get all cheeky with me, good sir."

"You are sweet like a sugar plum but stubborn as a kumquat. Don't get miffed. I'm kidding around with Miss Temperamental. At ease, private."

"Do I really have a disagreeable temperament?"

"Not in the least. Everything about you is perfection—except maybe for the fact that you do jump to conclusions."

She sat back and smiled. *So I am perfection, huh?* "I can't wait to set up the decorations we bought. Do you think they will deliver the sleigh and Santa tomorrow? It needs to look like it's flying."

"With certainty, yes," Chatwin responded.

"If only the good Lord will give us snow on Christmas day. Snow brings a feeling of a childhood fantasy coming to life. Don't you think?"

"I haven't thought about such things since... well, since years ago. I agree, though. Snow on Christmas is magical."

Suddenly, Chatwin heard the name "Tom Odell" announced over the radio.

He leaned forward and yelled, "Turn off that blasted radio, Jonesy, NOW! I can't hear myself think."

Talia looked at him with confusion. *Just what song does Tom Odell sing that he doesn't want to hear? I'll have to do some research.*

When they exited the car, Talia grabbed his hands in hers and said, "Thank you so much. I can't tell you how much this meant to me."

Unexpectedly, tears sprang to her eyes. Then she stood on her toes and kissed his lips, and the peck lingered.

He gently caressed her face and stared into her eyes before abruptly pulling away. "No, thank *you*. It has been a long time since I enjoyed a day of shopping—well, ever. My promise to you is that we shall do this more often."

Talia, Chatwin, and the rest of the staff congregated in the kitchen. Christmas butter cookies, pastries, and even figgy pudding were on the counter. Talia hugged Charles, Poppy, and Bertie.

"I'm so glad you're home, Poppy," Talia declared. "I missed you so much. And this smell brings back so many fond memories. When can we eat them?"

"I would hope now while they're warm," Charles replied.

"Besides, I knew you would want to watch *A Christmas Carol* this evening. I may just join you."

"You want to watch a Christmas movie with us?" Talia exclaimed. "Why, that's wonderful."

"I do believe you're becoming a softie, Charles," Chatwin said, smiling.

"Oh, shut up. All of you," Charles replied with his lips barely curving up. "And follow me into the family room."

Charles placed the trays of food next to the Christmas tree, which was decorated with old-fashioned ornaments, tinsel, and multi-colored lights. Poppy brought in a tray of hot cocoa, marshmallows, whipped cream, and cups.

"Everyone, please. Let's all sit down together, enjoy this moment, and cherish it the rest of our lives," Chatwin said.

Before the movie started, they sipped their cocoa and nibbled on the Christmas goodies as they talked and laughed. For Talia, it felt like a real Christmas with a real family.

"Now, bring us some figgy pudding," Talia sang. "The movie is beginning."

"I dare say, Charles. I hope you didn't over-egg the pudding like last year."

Charles sucked in his top lip and narrowed his eyes. With an hmmf spitting out of his mouth, he ran to the kitchen and was back in a jiffy with a tray of it.

"Charles, you did nothing wrong with this figgy. It is delicious."

During the film, Talia surveyed the room and smiled, seeing all the staff—including the ranch workers and yard staff sprawled about the room, watching the movie. *What a perfect Christmas,* she thought.

Chapter Seventeen

The next afternoon, Chatwin walked into the kitchen to find Talia and his staff covered with flour, powdered sugar, and food color dyes. It looked like a bomb had been set off in the kitchen.

"Blimey! Am I really in Charles' kitchen? The Charles I know would never allow such disarray and mess."

"Well, taste this, and then you'll understand why," Talia said as she pushed a cookie near his mouth.

The staff watched with silent anticipation as he took a bite. He wrinkled up his face with displeasure. Then, he said, "This is the *best* cookie I have tasted in my whole life."

Talia punched him in his abs. "You sneak. You had us fearful."

"After the day I've had, this is the perfect ending, except you better hide those cookies so I don't gain ten pounds by tomorrow."

"Oh, sir, even if you *did* gain ten pounds, you would still be handsome," Poppy said, laying a hand on Chatwin's shoulder.

Talia watched the exchanges between the beast, as she now referred to him with affection, and the staff. It wasn't like a normal lordship of a manor and staff arrangement. No, she decided, it *was* like being with a family. *He does treat his staff like they're family. They have a mutual respect and love for each other,* she thought.

"I certainly hope you all don't plan on leaving the cleanup to me alone," Charles commented sharply.

"No worries. We shall *all* help with the cleanup," Chatwin responded meekly.

"*You* will help?" Talia asked in shock.

"Why not? I don't mind getting messy in the right circumstances."

She gave Poppy a sly look, and Poppy shot her a knowing smile.

"Well, let's get to it then," Chatwin commanded agreeably.

As they cleaned, Talia threw a handful of flour at Chatwin. Poppy added a handful of powdered sugar, and kitchen war broke out. When it ended, they looked around, astonished at how much work they had ahead of them.

"Bertie, call 999 and inform them we have a hazmat incident. We clearly need the fire brigade for a disaster such as this," Chatwin said.

Bertie looked at Chatwin with trepidation.

"Take it easy, Bertie. I'm just jiving," Chatwin said with a laugh.

With a chuckle, Bertie replied. "Oh, yes. Good, Sir. Good one, sir."

It took a few hours, but Charles' kitchen was soon ready to be photographed in any magazine.

"Now that we're all exhausted, how about we all go out for pizza—after we shower and clean up, that is. Talia, please cover yourself well," Chatwin announced.

～

That night, Talia was sitting at her vanity, brushing her hair when Poppy strolled in. "Anything I can get for you or help you with, Lass?"

"Actually, yes. You can tell me what Christmas song causes the good sir such distress."

Poppy took the brush from her hand and brushed Talia's hair as she spoke. "Haven't we been through this enough, Lass? You know I'm not at liberty to discuss anything personal about our Lordship."

"Please, Poppy. I can't stand being in the dark. Please." Her face looked up at Poppy with determined pleading, and her mouth kept saying the word please without audibly speaking it.

"All right, Dear," Poppy whispered. "It is "Real Love." Don't even ask me why because I cannot tell you more. And if you dare betray my trust and mention it to him, it will be the last time I tell you anything, you little sneak." Poppy grabbed Talia's chin and squeezed it.

Talia reacted with a kiss to Poppy's cheek.

Chapter Eighteen

eading up to Christmas day, the staff buzzed with excitement. Talia learned that this Christmas season had been vastly different from the holidays in years past. The staff told her that the good sir had always been in a solemn mood during the holidays, so usually, the employees couldn't wait for Christmas to come and go.

"He's different this year," Poppy had confided in her. "He's happy. We're all happy, and we're so excited for Christmas day."

～

Everyone gathered in the family room on Christmas morning, drinking tea and eating a scrumptious bikky. Talia demanded, sweetly, of course, that they set up a couple of play pins for her mice and rabbits, who were dressed in Christmas outfits.

"I'll be right back," Talia said, and when she returned, she was wearing a one-piece, Christmas-designed pajama outfit. It looked like she walked off the set of *How the Grinch Stole Christmas.*

When Chatwin entered, Talia was disappointed to see that

he was still wearing those darn sunglasses, even though he donned a Christmas hoodie.

"Hello, all. Merry Christmas," Chatwin announced.

"It's about time you got here. It's time to open presents," Talia exclaimed with delight.

Chatwin announced that he gave all staff members a hefty bunce and tickets for a cruise in less than two weeks to Bora Bora. "That way, you'll be out of the way for the movers," he said.

"Oh, thank you, sir," Poppy commented.

"But that's not all," Chatwin said with a sly grin.

The staff couldn't hide their surprise as Chatwin passed out personal gifts for all of them.

Charles put his "Best Chef in the World" apron on with much pride and looked excitedly at the new cookware and utensils, picking each one up and admiring them like it was something sentimental.

Bertie dropped a few tears when he opened the picture frame with a photograph of him and Chatwin's parents.

Poppy squealed excitedly over her coffee maker and the beautiful China tea set.

The stable and groundskeepers held up their personalized initialed tools.

Jonesy tried on the exquisite sunglasses for every day of the week. He had a weakness for sunglasses.

Talia giggled with glee when she opened the DVD complete set of *Beauty and the Beast*. Then she froze on her second gift from the good sir when she pulled down the satin fabric, revealing a portrait of her with angel wings. In the painting, her hair and skin glistened with glitter, and the background appeared to be heaven. She was speechless.

Chatwin watched her reaction.

For the first time, everyone in the room, except Talia, noticed the angel topper on the tree. The sun shone brightly, illuminating its beauty, causing it to sparkle from the reflection of the sun. They had never noticed that one of the wings was missing a feather. They all looked curiously into each other's eyes.

"I have never seen anything so amazing. I only wish I were as beautiful as the woman in the painting. Thank you. From the bottom of my heart, thank you." She held the painting to her heart and smiled tearfully.

"Lass, the painting is an exact likeness of you in every way, wings and all," Chatwin said.

"Well, we all know I am far from being angelic. I have the temper of a serpent, I fear to admit."

"You're wrong. You have the temperament of an angel trapped in the body of a mortal."

"But why is a feather missing on one of the wings?" Talia asked.

"Because, Dearest, you are one feather short of becoming an angel."

She blushed. Then she opened the box that contained a ticket for the cruise. "Sir, you are letting me go on the cruise?"

"Yes. You deserve it. The whole staff will be accompanying you."

"And you as well?"

"Sorry, but someone has to manage the manor," Chatwin replied.

"You have to come. Please come," Talia begged.

"Now, now. Let's not ruin this most wonderful day with pouting. We can address this at a later time. Besides, I want to open *my* gifts."

He opened a gift from Talia. It was the figure of the beast from *Beauty and the Beast* wearing a hoodie. He chuckled. The next gift was another figure of the beast—except this one showed the beast transformed into the prince.

"So, is this what you really look like?" Talia asked him.

"Good try, Lass, but I'll never tell."

The prince wore a hoodie and sunglasses, but underneath, the doll was most handsome.

Next, Chatwin opened a gift from the whole staff. Bertie had set up a hidden camera to take a picture of them all when they were sitting in the family room covered in flour and whatnot, eating Christmas biccies. Then, he blew the photograph up and placed it in a frame with descriptive writing that said, "Our Family." Talia had held the good sir's hand as the picture snapped.

Seeing the framed photograph, Chatwin teared up and couldn't speak for a moment. Embarrassed by his emotional reaction, he dropped his head and spoke softly. "This is the greatest gift I have ever received. Thank you all so much."

Later, Charles prepared the best Christmas dinner of roast beef, Yorkshire pudding, roasted potatoes, and pan-roasted Brussels sprouts with streaky bacon and garlic. For sweet, he made a Christmas pudding and a Trifle.

Evening wear was required for the dinner. Talia wore a snug-fitting red dress that hung down her shoulders. Her shoes were a masterpiece—fit for a princess, red and glittery.

Chatwin swallowed excessively with his eyes glued to her. *She is exquisite*, he thought.

They ate and ate and ate. When they all finished, everyone cleaned up their own dishes and helped clean pots and pans, leaving a kitchen so sparkling that you could eat off the floor.

"The dog's bollocks, Charles. My, that was tasty," Chatwin expressed.

Charles nodded his thanks.

"Now, let's all retire to the family room for another movie," Chatwin said.

As they watched *Miracle on 34th Street*, Talia snuggled up next to Chatwin, leaning her head on his chest.

His heart rate accelerated, and he looked around, fearing the others could hear his heart's buh-bump, buh-bump sound. No one seemed to notice. He wanted to put his arms around her but sighed and decided that was a bad idea.

At the end of the evening, Chatwin looked around and saw that he was the only one awake. He laughed, surveying the staff snoring in various spots around the family room. Talia had fallen in his lap. Chatwin stroked her silky hair and gently caressed her cheek and arm. *Her scent is intoxicating. How much more of this can I take?* he thought.

Gently, he picked her up and carried her to her bed. As he pulled the blanket over her, she grabbed his hand and pulled him down to her. She lifted her head and kissed his lips with tenderness.

"Merry Christmas, Sweet One," he whispered, leaving the room.

Chapter Nineteen

The day after Christmas, the staff was still cheery, humming, skipping, and chatting gleefully. They were eating breakfast when Chatwin's stable groom strolled into the dining room.

Talia looked up as she took a spoonful of Weetabix.

"Well, you're late. You better sit down and eat before your meal gets cold," Chatwin demanded.

"Sir, could I speak with you in private? It is very serious."

Everyone watched with concern.

"Certainly. Let's step into the den," Chatwin said, standing.

In the den, the groom said, "The stables are starting to fall apart. I thought for sure you could hear the beams as they toppled on the ground. The waves have reached the stables, and part of the pasture is underwater. Sir, I've never seen anything like this since we've been here. We need to leave this estate —immediately."

"Arrangements have been made for the livestock. I will call and ask them to come out sooner and complete the move to Bibury while you all go on the cruise. It is a good that I already made arrangements to move the livestock. I admit that I've been feeling uneasy about these treacherous conditions as well."

"I am fearful that the whole manor will fall into the beastly sea any day, Sir."

"Why were you out there, anyway? There is nothing left for you to do."

"I had a few more saddles and tact to collect, but now everything is complete. All livestock are in the front pasture, away from the sea."

"Try not to worry," Chatwin told him with a pat. "If it turns for the worse, I'll send everyone to a hotel and get everything else moved."

"Yes, your Lordship. I'll keep you posted."

"Don't mention this to staff. We should have time before we need to abandon the manor, but I do not wish to alarm anyone. Come now and eat your brekkie."

"Aye, but I am starved."

As they reentered the dining room, everyone's eyes fell on Chatwin, trying to analyze his expression. Then, question after question arose. Chatwin finally informed everyone that he was keeping track of the sea. "If necessary, we will all stay in a hotel until the cruise. Now, not another word about it," he ordered.

Outside, the sea's roar magnified, and the wind wailed ferociously. Talia clutched the good sir for protection.

"No worries, Lass. I won't let that demon hurt hide nor hair of the likes of you all. I have professionals keeping an eye on the matter. Why our being here offends the sea so much is curious and irritating. Now, I don't want one worried face in this bunch. By now, it would seem you all know enough to trust me."

"Aye, good sir. But where will we live *after* our cruise?" Talia asked with concern.

"Remember when I told you to be careful what you wish for? Well, your wish of freedom may be the result of this dreadful situation."

"You mean, I may have my freedom?" she asked.

He simply nodded.

"Have I bored you to death with my presence? I am not a child. You don't have to treat me as such. I foolishly thought you enjoyed my company. Now you want to release me and be free of me? What am I missing? Just when I thought you were human, a man with human emotions and desires, that horrendous beast comes back to haunt me. Well, what are you waiting for? Release me now and be free of me once and for all."

As she turned and fled, Chatwin yelled, "Talia, wait!"

But the sound of her feet pounded up the stairs. Poppy followed her.

"I just can't figure her out," Chatwin told Bertie. "I thought the idea of freedom would make her merry. I give up. I'm retiring to my room. Unless it is a dire emergency, I wish to be left alone for the rest of the day."

In her room, Talia noticed that the heavy iron bars had been removed from the windows. Her hand went to her mouth in shock.

"Poppy. Poppy, where are you?"

"What's wrong, Child?"

"Poppy, please don't refer to me as a child."

"Forgive me, Miss. I have fond feelings for you as my very own child."

Talia's hands went up to her face with shameful eyes. "Do forgive me, Poppy.

I was overreacting to the—well, you know, and how he seems to dwell upon me as a child. I take offense to his childish treatment of me. I am a woman now, but I am not, in the least, offended by you calling me child—especially since you so fondly referred to me as your own daughter. Please, for my sake, never change that."

"You can be certain of that, my child."

Talia smiled affectionately.

"Now, what has you troubled so?"

"When were the iron bars removed from the windows? I just now noticed it."

"They were removed the day before Christmas. The good sir hired someone to remove them while you were out for a drive. He wanted to surprise you. I just figured you would notice all on your own."

"I'm so foolish. I have to thank him. I guess my whining is childish, to my shame." She took off for the kitchen, looking in every room for him.

"The good sir is in his chambers—not to be disturbed," Bertie told her.

"Well, I don't care. I have to thank him—for everything," Talia told Bertie, and she took off toward his chambers.

"Miss..." Bertie called, but she didn't look back.

Talia pounded on the door to his chambers. "Beast, Beast, I have to see you. Please open the door."

After a few minutes of pounding and yelling, the door opened.

She ran into his arms and sobbed. "I'm so sorry. I don't know what's wrong with me. I'm so thankful for all you've done."

"There, there. Please don't cry," he said, stroking her hair. "I had no intention of upsetting you. I thought my remarks would make you merry. But I must admit, I'm a bit offended that you're still calling me a 'beast.'"

"I'm sorry. It's just that I still don't know your real name, and I always resort to calling you a beast when I'm upset, but I was acting childish, thinking you were trying to get rid of me. I'm sorry. Believe it or not, I just noticed the bars removed from the windows. I feel like part of the family now, like you trust me and want me with you. Thank you so much. Those iron bars were a sad reminder of being a prisoner all these years, and now, I feel free. Thank you so much, my wonderful beast. It seems you have transformed from the beast just like the movie *Beauty and the Beast*—and the spell placed on you to make you kind and charming has been fulfilled."

"Actually, it *does* feel like we are living in a fairy tale. You are so enchanting. I fear heaven has been awaiting your return."

A sweet smile formed on her face. "Well, thank you. I do have an important request, though."

"And just would that be? I'm scared to ask."

"Please don't think of me as a child. I am a woman now. I would like to be treated and looked upon as such." Her eyes gleamed with mischief. Then she added, "Besides, I still have a sneaky suspicion that you are not much older than me."

"One day, you'll know the truth, but not tonight."

"Would you accompany me around the house outside? I want to see what a house—or castle looks like without iron bars."

"As you wish."

When they stepped outside, they detected an eeriness in the air. They both stood still, silent, listening. The crashing of the waves was closer, louder, and angrier. It was frightfully cold.

Fear riveted through Talia's body, but then she felt the light brush of an angel's wing on her cheek, and she immediately felt safe, leaning her head up toward heaven in wonder. *Thanks for the calming reminder that You are in control, Lord.* She glanced into the good sir's eyes, but his sunglasses made it impossible to see them.

Suddenly, they heard a loud crash as a piece of land slipped into the sea. The sound of falling rocks vibrated the ground beneath their feet as the waves roared, loud and intimidating. Talia held her breath in fear. He put his arm around her, and staff members ran out toward them, terror plastered over their faces.

"I shall call out the boffin first thing in the morrow. We will not fall into the sea this evening. Please calm down and trust me."

"I don't want to be alone this evening. I'm frightful," Talia said, snuggling into his embrace.

"Okay, Lass. We'll make up the couches and sleep there this evening. Good to go?"

"That sounds perfect."

Chapter Twenty

"I have good and bad news," the boffin informed Chatwin.

"Please, get to the point, then."

"I'd say you have weeks or possibly months before tragedy strikes the manor. It is not just this location feeling the powers of the sea. This is happening all around Europe. The whole area has received record amounts of rain and storm activity. It will settle down. I know it feels terrifying, but it *will* settle down eventually. However, I think you should consider making permanent living arrangements away from the sea because I don't know how long this crisis will last."

"But will the manor survive?" Chatwin asked him.

"That, I don't know. Let's face it. You have instigated this battle with the sea by building so close to the cliffs. Why did you do that? Do you think you have power over the sea?"

"Never mind all the speculation and insinuations, as if the sea were a living and breathing thing to negotiate with. That is simply preposterous. Maybe I was overly presumptuous to be that bold, but I do have a home elsewhere. I'll call you if I need your expertise anytime soon," Chatwin told him.

～

Reading a book, Poppy relaxed in a comfortable chair with her legs hanging over an ottoman as Talia scrolled the Internet searching for Tom Odell songs. When she found the song "Real Love," she clicked the link to read the lyrics, but instead, the song itself rang out loudly from the computer's speakers.

Unexpectedly, Chatwin walked in at that moment.

Poppy looked over at Talia with scornful, wide eyes.

"Turn that blasted radio off NOW!" Chatwin ordered sternly.

He turned and fled, and they heard his chamber door slamming. They listened in horror at the sound of crashing furniture and breaking glass.

"Poppy, what is it about this song that brings him to his knees? I didn't mean to play it. I thought I clicked on the lyrics. This Internet technology is still new to me. I promise you that it was not my intention to play it. Do you believe me?"

Poppy produced a sympathetic smile. "I believe you, but I'm sorry, Child. I am not able to discuss it—any of it. Please don't be offended. I would love to have another woman with whom to talk about the tragedies to which our Lordship has had to succumb, but alas, I cannot. Now, I think it would be good to retire to our rooms."

"As you wish. Thanks, Poppy. My heart breaks for him."

"As do all of our hearts. Don't allow your solicitous sincerity for him to cause you worry. All will work out. You'll see."

The next morning, Chatwin walked into the kitchen with a standoffish attitude.

The staff was silent.

"Can't any of you speak? Cat got your tongue? What?" Chatwin barked.

"Oh, sorry, good sir. I guess we're all pooped out from the holiday activities," Poppy said.

Everyone shook their heads in agreement, too scared to speak.

"Fine. I have a few meetings in town, and then a business trip is scheduled for a day."

Talia's shoulders slumped. She wanted to spend time with him today.

"Sir, would it be convenient for me to walk you to the car?" she asked.

"Why? Do you have a problem you need to speak to me about?" he responded curtly.

"No. Not at all. I just want to walk you to the car. Is that some sort of crime?"

"I don't have time for dramatics. We'll talk when I return."

"Or maybe NOT!" Talia yelled.

"Tell me, do you wish to be treated like an adult or child? Think that through before answering."

"Why, you pompous, treacherous egomaniac."

"Just as I thought," Chatwin said. "Don't forget to place a bib on the child before she drools food onto her clothes."

Fury washed over Talia's expression. "And whatever you do, hide those bones in his room before they are found. You wouldn't want someone to find out a *beast* lives here!" She stomped out of the room.

The staff sat with their heads down, statuesque. When Chatwin raced after Talia, Bertie, and Poppy jumped up from their chairs to stare out the window. Suddenly, Charles was beside them, also looking. Bertie and Poppy glanced at him with surprise.

"What?" Charles asked. "I just want to see what all the commotion is about. The way you two are acting, you'd think he is strangling the lass." He shrugged his shoulders and went back into the confines of the kitchen.

Chatwin caught up with Talia and grabbed her arm. "You just stop right now. Do not defy me, or I will make your life most miserable."

She put her index finger to her mouth and formed a look of

deep thought. "Let's see. I am a prisoner. I'd say that already qualifies as a miserable life."

"Oh, so now you're miserable?" Chatwin asked. "Days ago, you were crying because I suggested giving you your freedom. Make up your mind!"

"I should think not. It is a woman's prerogative to change her mind. My *mind* thinks you have turned back into the beast. Now, if you don't mind, Sir, I will retire to my room so I can escape your awful monster smell." She pinched her nose together and walked off.

He grabbed her arm again and swung her around to face him. "You will not speak to me like that!"

His grip was hurting her, and for a moment, her face flashed with fear. Then, her temper overrode her trepidation. "I know you must be a hungry beast, but I fear you wouldn't like my flavor, Sir. My meat would be tough and chewy because of all the hardships I have endured—from *you*. Please go find some other poor creature to satisfy your hunger."

His face turned red with fury. Then, suddenly, he busted out into laughter.

Talia laughed, too, and then he drew her into his arms and kissed her aggressively. Then, the kiss softened, and he cupped her face in his hands, gently planting kisses all over her face.

She felt dizzy, then angry, desiring more intimacy but holding back. "Don't stop. Please don't ever stop."

Once again, he came to his senses and pulled back abruptly. "I'm sorry. I didn't mean"—

"No. No. It's okay. I'm not upset. Can't you see how happy I feel?"

"Good evening, Sweet One. I must go." He turned and ran to the car, yelling for Jonesy.

As she watched him drive away, she spoke aloud to herself. "What is wrong with me? Has my mind warped into some kind of lovesick girl that I will settle for a life of 'Does he love me or does he not' ridiculousness? I can't take it anymore. Quit acting like some silly schoolgirl!" she scolded herself.

"Oh, Poopy, darling. Where are you?"

Talia didn't want Bertie to know she was listening, but she couldn't help herself and stuck her head outside the door to hear the sweetness. She smiled at his affectionate words.

The day Bertie mistook Poppy's name for "Poopy" ended up being a change in direction for their relationship—and his new nickname obviously stuck. Talia stepped out, peeked around the corner, and saw Bertie give Poppy a peck on the cheek. Poppy blushed with fondness and caressed his hands.

"A romance in the making. My, they are adorable together," she remarked in a melancholy mood. "If only I had a romance so sweet."

Chapter Twenty-One

"Poppy! Bertie! Charles! I'm scared. Can't you hear the crashing of the waves over the land?" Talia shouted.

The urgent sound of footsteps came quickly. "It will be okay, child," Poppy assured her.

"The good sir will not let harm come to us. That, you can be sure of," Bertie added.

"I agree, but I must admit. I have never heard the sea so vocal and so close to us as it is now. If I am being truthful, I am startled by the recent events that the sea has caused," Charles added.

"Look. All livestock is about to be removed. There are several ranch hands out there, as we speak. We'll discuss the latest threats with him when he returns. For now, let's all camp out in the family room," Bertie suggested.

"But what about Flipflops and TippyToes?" Talia asked.

"Didn't the good sir tell you?" Poppy asked with arched eyebrows.

"Tell me what?"

"Your rabbits will be taken to safety soon. He also has hired someone specifically to tend to them."

Talia smiled and sighed with relief. Then, fear washed over

her face once again. "But, what if that's too late? Just listen to the treacherous sea. I fear for their lives right *now*."

Just then, one of the ground's staff walked in holding two pet carriers. He lifted them up and asked, "Where shall I put Toetips and Floppyflip?"

Everyone in the room broke out in laughter.

"Am I the only one who will ever get their names right?" She laughed harder.

"In the family room, please," Bertie responded.

"Thank you all for catering to my most precious possessions," Talia said.

"You're most welcome, and before you ask, Tidbit and family are already in the family room," Bertie informed her with an affectionate smile.

"Living here all these years, having to figure out for myself what your faces are hiding, I am pretty sure I now know what profession to go into."

At this point, everyone in the room faced her dying to find out what conclusion she came to.

"A behaviorist. I'm sure you all would agree," she remarked, looking into each one of their eyes with a one-sided pucker to her mouth.

~

Later, Bertie called Chatwin to discuss the perilous conditions of the sea. Chatwin was extremely frustrated. It would be months before the remodel on the new house was complete, but he knew that if he had to move the household in early, he'd do it. Their safety was of utmost importance.

The next morning, he returned to the manor early and found everyone asleep in the family room.

"Well, why wasn't I invited to this campout?" he asked.

Bertie jumped up in a daze. "Oh, good sir. I hadn't expected you home this early. We'll see to breakfast and the day's activities."

"Not so fast. Sit. Go on. Sit back down, all of you. Now, what is the meaning of this campout?"

"Sir, as I spoke to you over the phone regarding the raging sea, I fear we all were spooked and decided to spend our evening together," Bertie told him.

"I see. Even the mice joined the fun."

"And the rabbits," Talia added. "I couldn't leave them outside or alone in my room, Sir. What if the waves crashed through the tower?"

"Of course, you couldn't. You would never forgive yourself if they were in fear for their lives," Chatwin said with sarcasm.

"This is true," Talia said earnestly.

"Well then, I have the boffin on the way. How about we all make some pancakes?"

Charles shook his head. "Please, can we keep it from turning into a bombsite?"

"Of course, Charles. Of course." Chatwin patted him on the shoulder as they all worked excitedly to make a delectable breakfast. "Oh, I forgot. I thought we would try this breakfast coffee. The flavor sounds intriguing." He plopped the grocery bag on the counter.

"In place of tea, Sir?" Charles wrinkled up his nose, asking.

"You bet. Now, off with those it-has-to-be-tea faces. Let's live a little spontaneously for a change."

"Yes, sir," Charles replied, sounding like Eeyore from *Winnie the Pooh*.

Talia chuckled with delight.

After breakfast, Chatwin announced, "I'm off to scout the cliffs."

"Would it be okay if I accompany you to the cliffs, sir?" Talia requested. "It's just that I am fearful and would like to see it for myself. With you there, I feel safe."

"That will be fine, but you need to stay near me. I don't want a wave or strong wind to knock you over the cliff. The wind is most forceful today. Warning alerts have been blasting through the radio all the drive here."

"I shall be careful. I'll run and change," she said.

"Good to go."

"Good to go, sir."

With the rainy conditions, Chatwin drove them to the cliffs in a terrain vehicle. The inspector was waiting, pacing back and forth. As they approached him, Talia heard the inspector exclaim, "Does he think he is the only person in the world? I have many stops to make before the day ends. Jerk!"

By his grumbling, it was difficult to believe Chatwin and the inspector were great friends.

"It's about time you sorry—excuse me, ma'am. I wasn't aware that a woman as beautiful as you would be in the company of this selfish beast."

Chatwin laughed with vigor. "You old goat. Quit your faffing around. You're always grumbling about something. What happened to Thomas?"

"He called and said he couldn't make it."

"Fine. Let's get down to business. This is my guest. Just call her Miss."

The inspector kissed her hand and stared at her like she was a ghost.

Chatwin waved his hands around his face. "I knew it. You can cast spells. Look at him. He's hypnotized."

"You better take that back. I cannot cast spells. I am not a—"

"Calm down," Chatwin said gently, pushing on her shoulders. "Once again, you can't take a joke."

"I can't tell when you're kidding or when you're serious."

"This time, I'm just kidding. Arley, snap out of it," Chatwin said.

"Please forgive me, Miss. It's just...it's just that I have never seen anyone so captivating and enchanting. What are you doing with this jerk?"

She didn't know how to respond.

Chatwin looked at Talia. "Stay here." Then, to Arley, he said, "Come with me." As they walked, Chatwin whispered, "Do not call me by my name. I am still in hiding, and she would recognize my name." Then, he raised his voice to a normal conversational tone. "Now, would you mind getting on with your findings?"

"Sure, but first, what's the deal with the angel?" Arley asked, nodding his head toward Talia.

"Forget you ever saw her, and never bring her up to anyone. She is hiding, likewise. You would be the only person on the outside to know of her presence. If word gets out, I will know it is by you."

"Your secret is safe with me. We've been friends far too long for me to do something so stupid. Now, you're not going to like my findings."

Chatwin formed a frown and blew out a disgusted sigh.

"The waters are rough today. Listen to the waves clamoring against the cliffs. Whoa! Did you see those waves come up over the cliff? The wind is more powerful than I've ever seen it." He automatically stepped back a few paces.

Chatwin looked over at where Talia was standing a few feet away. Fright glistened in his eyes. She was too close to the edge. "Come back," he yelled.

But the wind was so loud, she could not hear him. Without warning, a violent wave crashed over the cliff, knocking her to the ground. Then, as part of the cliff started giving away, she was being pulled with it. She screamed.

Chatwin ran like a race car to Talia, who was now dangling over the rocky, unstable cliff. Arley caught up to them, and both men grabbed each of Talia's hands, pulling her to safety. Chatwin carried Talia far away from the cliff.

"I'm sorry to have put you both in danger," Talia said.

"*Us?* You put *yourself* in danger. Don't you ever go that close to the cliff again. Do I make myself clear?" Chatwin demanded. "In fact, don't you ever, ever come here again. It is not safe!"

She didn't know how to react, so she did nothing.

"Hey, we're okay. You need to calm down there, ole chap," Arley said, coaxing Chatwin's hand off Talia. "You're going to frighten her more. She didn't mean for it to happen."

Talia stood silent, too scared to move.

"It's—It's just that—" he was having a hard time speaking. "She could have been killed. The thought terrifies me."

Her tender eyes looked up at him. "I'm really sorry, and I promise you I will never do something that stupid ever again."

"Good. Now, let's continue with the report," he said to Arley.

"As you can see for yourself, the conditions have changed. You should be totally moved out of this place within two to three weeks."

"I'm working on that."

"Is she part of your staff?" he asked, looking at Talia. "Are you living together or something?"

"What did I tell you, Ar? It's complicated, but she will be moving with the rest of us until she decides she has had enough of us."

Her mouth dropped, and she looked at him with uncertainty. "What are you saying?"

"Not now. Please. We'll discuss it later. Now, I'm going to get you back so you can change into dry clothes and be warm and comfy. Thanks, Arley."

"Yeah, sure. Hey, you coming to the poker game this coming weekend?" Arley asked.

"I have too much going on. I think I'll skip it."

"I'd skip it too if I had the opportunity to spend time with the likes of her," Arley said with a smile.

Chatwin chuckled as they shook hands and departed.

Later, Talia entered the family room wearing a warm, floor-length nightgown.

"Hey," Chatwin said. "We're about to have a meeting. Will you join us? It concerns you, as well. I wish I had booked that cruise for today instead of New Year's, but what's done is done. I will have you all pack up the rest of the estate, and I will also bring in help to load it onto the moving trucks. I'd like everything to be packed up by the end of this week. You can enjoy the cruise while I set up temporary arrangements for a cottage on the outskirts of Wales. Unfortunately, the work on our new home is taking longer than our agreement. Please be patient with me and understand this will take time, but it *is* in the works as we speak. You will all be pleased."

Chatwin stared into Talia's eyes, which were expressionless.

"Now, Talia, your pets will have to live in cages temporarily until our permanent residence is completed, but they will be roomy and comfy for your critter friends."

"Thank you, Sir. That means a lot."

"As you all must understand, I must maintain business as usual. I do have a hearty income I need to keep up to help house the likes of you all." A smile smirked across his face. "Happily, I'll add. More boxes will arrive tomorrow, so I ask you all to be diligent and pack as quickly as possible. I would never be able to live with myself if anything horrid happened to any of you in my care."

The gardener hung his head. He had created a masterpiece in landscaping. Now, it would be destroyed.

Seeing his long face, Chatwin pulled him into a one-arm hug. "You will love our new grounds, but they need your touch to make them extra special."

Talia's eyes blurred with tears, seeing how he cared for his staff.

"Now, now. Don't let this vicissitude bring you down. Don't

be so glum. We will all be together, and I promise not one of you shall feel regret when you see what is in store."

Talia looked at him and said, "I...uh... oh, never mind. It's a stupid question."

"Go ahead. Let's hear it," he encouraged with a smarmy guise.

"When you said I can bring my critters, you are referring to—"

"—ToeTips and FlopsFlip—or whatever you call them—may come too. Actually, I have everything set up for them. I forgot to mention that."

She snickered, covering her mouth with her hand; he would never get the rabbits' names correct. Ever.

"Now, I must pack and leave for a board meeting. I'll be back in a day. Leave my room alone. I will pack my things when I return."

"Yes, good sir," Bertie formally replied.

"Everyone good to go?"

"They all shook their heads and replied in unison: "Good to go, sir."

Chapter Twenty-Two

"Tell Charles not to fix supper. I'm picking up some pizzas. He'll just have to suffer at the flavors and preparation by other hands, Bertie," Chatwin instructed him over the mobile.

"Be certain he will, good sir. Looking forward to having you home."

"As am I. We still have a home, right?"

"Yes, sir. It has settled down somewhat while you have been away." *It seems the sea is at peace when he is out of town,* Bertie thought. *How odd.*

"Good to go. See you momentarily."

When Chatwin entered the front door, all the staff and Talia stood at attention to welcome him home.

"Why so formal? Relax. This is making me uncomfortable. I'm not used to my staff showing such formality."

Talia couldn't get her hand to her mouth before a giggle escaped.

"Sir, we are just happy you are home," Bertie replied.

Jonesy carried in a pile of pizzas and laid them on the dining room table.

"I have a special treat. Hot fudge sundaes for sweet," Chatwin announced.

Talia grinned like a child while clapping her hands together.

"Let's eat everyone," Chatwin demanded, showing his affection for them in his smile. He peeked into rooms as he passed them. "Wow! You have been busy packing. Good job by all."

"Aye, good sir. We have it almost packed up," Poppy replied proudly.

"Is there anyone in the whole wide world who has the kindest, most efficient staff than I do? I should say not."

~

Everyone watched Charles devour the pizza with gusto. They tried to control their laughter, turning their faces in different directions from him and covering up their laughter with coughs. When Talia snorted, trying to hold back her laugh, he looked up and followed the trail of faces.

"Have you never seen a man eat before?" he grumbled. "I worked my bum off today. I happen to be famished. It may not be the best of flavors, but my stomach is in need of nutrients, this greasy mess and all."

The laughter was just what everyone needed. Even Charles broke down in a boisterous laugh, which was uncommon for him.

After an hour, Talia spoke up. "Well, that ice cream isn't going to scoop itself. Who will join me in delighting our taste buds with flavors that will explode inside our mouths?"

"Oh, blimey. It's brass monkeys outside. Wouldn't you prefer some hot tea and crumpets?" Charles asked pompously.

"Really, Charles? Do not act the part of a grockel. If we waited for warm weather in this region, we would never be allowed to eat anything cold. Enjoying a cold sweet on a cold winter's day is not uncommon. I should help the lass. Now, should I surprise you, Charles? Or will you be so kind as to inform me what kind of ice cream you would like?" Chatwin asked.

Charles stared straight in front of him with his arms crossed, defiance beaming on his face.

With a grizzle, Poppy briskly stated, "Charles, do not kerfuffle over such absurdities as ice cream on a cold winter's day." Poppy retreated to a pouting stance as his.

"Do you have Cornish clotted cream or razzle dazzle?" Charles finally asked.

"Aye, both," Chatwin replied.

"Cornish clotted cream and no topping is necessary," Charles said sullenly.

"Poopy," Chatwin said, and he chuckled before finishing his sentence. "What would you like?"

"Razzle dazzle, of course, with just a hint of raspberry cream, if you have it."

Chatwin took the rest of the orders, and Talia went into the kitchen to help him prepare them. While Chatwin was preparing the bowls of delight, Talia tried to force a large clump of ice cream into her small mouth. Chatwin fell onto the counter, laughing so hard, tears fell down his face. "Oink, oink," he managed to say before falling back down on the counter in hysterics.

Talia used her spoon as a slingshot, which sprayed ice cream onto his face. "Oink, oink yourself," she said.

He stood straight with no emotion whatsoever and remarked with a pococurante demeanor, "You know what this means, don't you?"

"I fear I have no idea what you're talking about." She stood in a face-off with him and showed no signs of retreat.

He scooped ice cream into a baseball, molding it but not packing it firmly. Then, he sprayed whipped cream all over it, and with a pitcher performance, he threw it at her. It fell apart all over her pajamas.

Her mouth dropped. She really didn't think he would throw it.

"Oh, that's it," she yelled, grabbing some ice cream with her hands and blasting him like throwing grenades.

After raising their tea towels as surrender flags above the kitchen island, they caught their breaths from laughing so hard. Then, they hurried to fill the bowls with whatever they could salvage.

"Maybe they had to run to the store for the ice cream," Poppy said, puzzled, wondering what could be taking them so long.

When Chatwin and Talia brought out the bowls and handed them out, the staff looked at each other in shock.

"Did you mean to give the mice and critters these bowls?" Bertie asked, confused.

"Certainly, this is a joke," Charles grumbled.

"I...uh... I just thought everyone was so full, so I decided to just give each of us a taste until we are hungry enough for more," Chatwin explained sheepishly.

"Poppycock! You can't do something this simple? I'll do it myself. Give me your bowls," Charles snapped.

"No!" Chatwin and Talia yelled in unison, knowing Charles would never survive the mess they made in the kitchen.

"We...uh... they didn't give us enough ice cream, but I've ordered some more, and it should arrive within minutes. I do, however, still have plenty of this ice cream," Chatwin said, holding up a bowl. "Jonesy, I got this especially for you. Let me know what you think."

"Sir, I am just plain gobsmacked. This is peanut butter and whiskey, is it not?" Jonesy enquired.

"You guessed it," he answered.

Just then, Charles noticed the stains of ice cream, fudge, and whipped cream all over Chatwin and Talia's clothes. Her fingers rubbed the smears as though trying to make them disappear. Then the staff noticed Chatwin, who was also fidgeting to hide the many spots on his clothes. As Talia reached up to remove the sticky strands of hair glued to her face and eyes, she crinkled her face with distaste at the feel of the sticky mess.

Chatwin tried with all his might not to expose his laughter at Talia's face of disgust, watching her open and close her sticky fingers.

"I am not a stupid man. I know what's happening, and my kitchen better not be a mess," Charles declared.

Talia and Chatwin smiled knowingly. *Good thing the good sir called a cleaning crew already,* Talia thought.

Before Chatwin could respond to Charles, the doorbell rang. "I'll get it," Chatwin remarked a little too eagerly.

As Chatwin answered the door, Charles asked, "What is all that clanging?" He rose to head into the kitchen.

"There was a leak, so the good sir called a plumber," Talia replied.

"Why would a leak even matter?" Charles asked haughtily. "Everything will all be destroyed in months anyway. Besides, I have never noticed a leak."

"Just let it go, would you, Charles?" Chatwin said as he returned with the ice cream.

"As you wish, sir. I'll get some new bowls," Charles replied.

"No!" Talia yelled. "Let me do that. Charles, you just relax. You do so much for us," she said as she hurried toward the kitchen.

Poppy looked at Bertie and whispered, "I think they are trying to keep Charles from the kitchen, and I bet I know why."

Bertie smiled in knowing agreement.

After getting everyone new ice cream, Charles seemingly forgot about the kitchen for a while.

"This is so good," Talia said, taking a big bite of her dessert. Then, something soft and fuzzy crawled on Talia's leg. She let out a short "Eeek" and looked down to see her mouse. "Tidbit, what in the world are you doing here? Oh! I forgot to put you back into your home." She held him and kissed his head.

"Do you think he will let me hold him?" Chatwin asked eagerly.

"Well, I'm sure he would," she replied enthusiastically.

"Wait, I want to win his trust. I'll be right back." He jogged back into the room with blueberries and seeds. As Chatwin coaxed the mouse with food, Tidbit crawled slowly onto Chatwin's hands. Chatwin rubbed the fur between Tidbit's ears. "I do admit that he is cute—for a mouse."

When Charles finished his ice cream, he returned to his original thought. "I hope my kitchen is not a pigsty." Charles just had to end the conversation with his usual grouchy manner.

Talia whispered to Chatwin, "Do you think they're done?"

"I don't know. It was a mess. There was even ice cream on the ceiling, but I don't hear any noise anymore," Chatwin replied.

"That's it. You're not keeping me out of my kitchen any longer. I must see what the two of you are hiding," Charles said, standing and walking toward the kitchen.

Talia and Chatwin followed him, relieved to see that the kitchen was spotless.

Talia smiled up at Chatwin. "That was a close call,"

"It was," he replied.

"Would you want to stroll around the yard and look at the stars?" Talia asked him. "I'm feeling a little gutted about leaving this piece of utopia."

"Well, I'll admit to being a little knackered, but I think it would be pleasant. Bundle up, and I'll meet you by the terrace doors," Chatwin replied.

Chapter Twenty-Three

Talia returned Tidbit to his family, and then she donned her winter attire. When she entered the family room, she saw Chatwin jump up from the couch and rub his eyes.

"Were you asleep?" she asked him.

"Just resting my eyes."

"Oh, dear me. I didn't realize how exhausted you are. We can do this another time. You get some rest."

"Don't be silly. I'm good to go." He threw on a warm coat over his hoodie and held the door open for her. A swish of cold wind blew in, and they both shivered. "We'll be fine," he said.

They walked along the breathtaking grounds of splendor. Even in the wintertime, the landscaping beamed with pride.

"Listen," she said.

"I don't hear a thing."

"Exactly. I think the sea finally took a nap. She must be tuckered out with all the racket and activity lately. The rain usually stops in December, but not this year."

"You continue to amaze me. How is it you know so much about everything? I have never met a soul as observant as you."

"I learn most things from my studies. Plus, I find the weather interesting."

"You find everything interesting."

"Aye, but I do. If people only knew what a wonderful and whacky world we live in, they would show more interest in our world. Maybe it's because my life has been so confined. If I were home, it would undoubtedly be all about boys."

"You say that, but I remember you..."

"You remember what?"

"I was going to say I remember you saying something about not being interested in boys when you were younger."

Even in the cold air, perspiration beaded on his forehead, but thankfully, the hoodie shielded it.

"True. But I did tell you that I often dreamt about this boy named Chatwin. He was the only one. But now that I have grown, I *am* interested in boys. I want to find out everything about them."

"Whoa! Slow down there, Lass."

"I didn't mean that—well, I *do* want to find out about men intimately—but one man—and in wedlock. I came this far being a virgin. I daresay I shall die a virgin."

"Let's not get dramatic. I think we should change the subject."

They found some huge rocks and sat down, staring up at the stars.

"Do you see that little cluster of stars right there?" she asked, pointing.

"There are a million star clusters."

"No, no, no. One cluster is brighter and twinkling like it wants us to notice it. Follow my finger and look." Then she grabbed his hand and pointed his index finger in the right direction.

"Hhhh!" he gasped. "You're right. It is brighter and twinkles more than the others. How peculiar."

"I believe that's the entrance to heaven."

"It is curious. But look over there." He grabbed her finger and pointed.

"Oh, my goodness! The stars are formed like a heart shape. How is that possible?"

"That is exactly what I wanted you to see," he said in wonder.

"The good Lord is obviously trying to get our attention. Hi, up there, Lord," she yelled sweetly.

"It's not that I don't believe in God, but I feel He has abandoned me and taken a disliking to me," Chatwin said, suddenly serious.

"If anyone should feel that way, it is I—but I don't. He is just as magnificent as always. If I'm being honest, I guess I have felt abandoned also, until I realized that something good comes out of tragedy for all His children. I know something good is going to happen. 'When' is the keyword."

"I admire you—for what you have been through—the loneliness, the neglect, and the abuse, and still, you find the good in things and still have faith. How did you get to be that way?"

"God is all I had to rely on for years. I fear living in these surreal conditions has taken my eyes off Him. When we have no one, we seek Him with our hearts and long for Him. Plus, my Sunday school teachings stuck with me."

He squeezed her hand. "You are truly an angel sent from heaven. He must be overjoyed with you."

"I doubt that. As you well know, I have quite the temper and speak my mind."

"Aye, you do." He chuckled heartily. "But it is the temperament of an angel. For heaven's sake, you even sparkle like an angel." They were quiet for a few moments, and then he asked, "Why is it you sparkle, do you suppose?"

"That's easy. When I was born, my mum said heaven's dew gathered around any place I went. It always showed up wherever I traveled. I don't know why. One evening—how I got abducted in the first place, and I think I told you this part before—I looked out my bedroom window. I couldn't sleep, and everyone had gone to bed, so it was dark as tar. A bright, sparkly trail led to my rowboat. I was so curious that I ran and jumped in it. The river sparkled like never before, and I followed the path.

"I took my time and sniffed the fragrant flower blooms and even picked them. It was like every step I took shined like daylight. But one particular path on the river twinkled and grew brighter. I rowed until the path went up onto dry land. There was a sign with the name 'Cordina'."

He gasped in silence, too confounded to speak.

"Following the spectacular, glittery path, it led me to this place that looked like heaven on earth. There was a pond that flowed into the Coln, but a special little pond was inside the bigger pond. When I bent over, the watery substance was thick and sparkled with magical colors. I put some in my hand and watched with bewilderment. It even had a mild vibration. The smell and taste were like manna from heaven—not that I know what manna smells or tastes like. It was the perfect sweetness of nectar and honey.

"After I started tasting it, my body, face, and hair started to sparkle. I just hope it wasn't some radioactive goop that will kill me in the end. As far as I know, nobody has ever found it. I pray the area has not been developed. That will be my home one day, and no one will ever know of its existence. I feel in my soul that it is a gift from the Lord above to me, who will cherish and guard it until the end of the world."

"Have you ever acted out a Shakespearean play? You would get a standing ovation."

"Are you mocking me, sir?"

"Not in the least. It is a compliment. Maybe that cluster of stars is made up of angels. It looks as though God put a million of you together in one cluster."

"Now you're embarrassing me."

"Are you really that blind to your beauty and charm?"

"If you must know, yes, I am. There is far more to a person

than looks. If I am beautiful, as you say, then I fear it is a curse. Look where it has gotten me. I guess beauty deserves such an appalling and lonely life. People can only see the outward beauty. If there is no inward beauty, what good is it? It is an offense and nothing more."

"My, you're dramatic and full of wisdom. You need not worry. Your inward beauty is what makes you sparkle."

"Thank you. I can't even form the right words to show how much I appreciate your kind words. Now, *that* is what I call a compliment. Thank you, good sir."

"I've been meaning to ask you about your father," Chatwin asked, changing the subject.

"What is it you wish to know?"

"What type of man is he? I have heard rumors that he is a drunk."

Her fiery eyes stared at him. "How dare you! I never *ever* saw my father with a bevy. I know he drank, but Mum said he gave it up altogether—that was just before my abduction." She snapped her fingers. "Just like that. Now that I am older, it seems a little odd that he stopped so abruptly. I wonder if there was a reason. Anyway, that is a very callous thing for you to say. It's just despicable."

"Please accept my apology. It was an unfortunate choice of words."

"Apology not accepted!" She pushed her body up and began to walk away, but a huge, powerful wave crashed eight feet out in front of them, close enough to splash over them. They were both soaked.

"It's getting worse." Chatwin's face filled with fear. "And you're freezing. Let's get you into the manor," he said, putting his arms around her.

Chapter Twenty-Four

As the morning sun beamed through the curtains, the intercom buzzed loudly. Bertie rushed to answer it quickly before it woke Chatwin.

"May I help you?" he asked in his usual, professional butler tone.

"I'm here to meet with Chatwin. He phoned me last night to conduct an inspection of the grounds. He said it is quite urgent."

"Oh. I see," Bertie replied, and he opened the gates. After showing the visitor to the parlor, Bertie said, "I'll see if the good sir is ready to see you. Please wait here." He quickly walked up the stairs and knocked on Chatwin's door.

"I'm up, Bertie. Has my guest arrived?'

"Yes, good sir."

"I'll be down momentarily. Please fix him a spot of tea."

"Aye, good sir," Bertie said, closing Chatwin's door behind him. To the visitor, he said, "Please follow me and have a spot of tea. The good sir will be down shortly."

The visitor wrinkled up his face. "Good sir! Is that what you call the ole Chat?"

Bertie paused at the foot of the stairs. As he turned to look at the gentleman, his face contorted to annoyance, but before Bertie could reply, Chatwin met them at the base of the stairs.

"I'll handle this, Bertie. Thank you." Chatwin patted Bertie's shoulder affectionately.

The man jumped up and shook Chatwin's hand, smiling. "Well, look at you, your majesty."

"Enough of the sarcasm," Chatwin replied. "Look, I need you to *not* call me by my name. Period. It's very important. Call me Kendrick like you did when we were children."

His guest's eyes widened, and he tilted his head back. "What's going on?"

"I have no the time to speak with you about it, Thomas. Let's just get right down to business."

"Why in the heck are you wearing a disguise in your own house? Out in town, I understand, but here..." Thomas asked.

"Like I said..."

A powerful crash caused the windows to shake. Talia ran down the stairs, missing a step and falling straight into Chatwin's arms.

"Oh, sir, forgive me. That crash gave me such a fright."

She suddenly realized that she had forgotten to put on her robe, and instinctively, her arms wrapped around her breasts. She bit her bottom lip in embarrassment for coming downstairs in her nightgown.

"Who do we have here, you sly devil?" Thomas asked.

"She is a guest and nothing more, so drop the whole scandal in your dirty mind. Talia, please meet Thomas."

Thomas extended his hand and smiled mischievously.

She stared at his face with narrowed eyes. She wasn't certain if she liked this bloke or not. Then she retracted her hand with quickness and re-crossed her arms because his eyes were drifting to uncomfortable areas.

"Thomas is going to inspect the cliff, or what is left of it, to see how much time we must get out before it all collapses. Please run along and get yourself dressed."

Talia formed a fake smile and backed up to the stairs. Then, she quickly turned around and ran up to the tower stairs.

"Where on earth did you find her? Out of a storybook?" Thomas asked.

"We're just friends. She's getting ready to move into her permanent home."

"You're not dating her?" Thomas' lip curved up with astonishment.

"No, I'm not, and neither will you."

"Come on. Why can't I ask her out? You're lying. I can tell you have feelings for her."

Chatwin's voice rose. "You don't know what you're talking about. I need you to not speak of her to anyone. She is in hiding, and I can't tell you why. I called you because we were —and *are*, I hope, still best friends. I thought you were someone I could count on to keep this quiet. Can I count on you?"

"Of course. I've kept the secret of you being in hiding all of these years—even before you grew all that hair. Your assistant is most capable in handling your affairs, Chat, ole boy."

"I told you not to call me by my first name."

"Of course, your majesty. I will keep it quiet. Besides, you have helped me out of some horrific financial decisions and showed me the way to prosperity. I would be homeless if it wasn't for you. And I'm pretty sure you plan to pay me dearly for my services, as usual?" He tipped his head and pushed his eyebrows up and down.

"I can't tell if we're really friends or if you like using my situation as blackmail."

"That's offensive. Have I ever asked you for more money?"

Chatwin lowered his head, biting his lower lip. "Sorry, friend. You have always been nothing more than a friend. I'm just saying that I'm sure my generous payment has a way of making it an even closer friendship."

"Ah, come on," Thomas said, waving his hand.

"We don't have time to waste. Let's go out to the cliffs so you can inspect them."

Thomas grabbed a biccie and plopped it into his mouth on their way out the door. As they walked, he looked back, tilting his eyes upward at the tower to see Talia watching them, her eyes sparkling. "Is she a fairy or something?" Thomas asked.

"Why do you ask such codswallop?" Chatwin retorted with a shake of his head.

"Just look at her. She is breathtaking and...and purely fascinating. Magnificent."

Chatwin followed Thomas' eyes up to the tower. He almost gasped from her beauty. "Oh, you mean the shimmering," Chatwin said. "She explained that she drank some strange substance, which started the iridescence. Anyway, she *is* spectacular, but she is also pure as a babe. I would kill anyone who dared to take her innocence away. Anyone!" His teeth grinded, and his eyes narrowed with constricting pupils.

Holding his hands up, Thomas said, "I get it. Don't worry about me. I get it. You still a champion in street fighting and martial arts?" he asked, backing away.

"Yes. I've surpassed the black belt. I train four to five times a week—in martial arts and street fighting. It gives me something to do and helps suppress my temperament's fury.

"Gooood to know, Bud."

"Now, quit chatting, and come on," Chatwin remarked gruffly.

At the cliffs, Thomas walked around, performed some calculations, and wrote up his summary. With a worried look, he approached Chatwin. "Hey, Man, you need to move soon. It's not safe. Remind me. Why did you build so close to the cliff?"

Chatwin's eyes flamed. "It's not like I anticipated this would happen. It's relaxing to hear the sea below crashing against the rocks, but now, they're fighting the cliff as though they were mortal enemies."

Thomas backed away from him again. "I understand."

When they returned to the manor, they saw livestock trucks driving down the driveway. The trailers rattled all the way to the stables. Chatwin noted his staff directing them where to park while others led horses out of the stable onto trailers.

"Oh, look. Your mistress—I mean your guest is running out to the stables. She looks distressed," Thomas said, pointing.

He glared at Thomas with eyes of fire. Thomas reached up with his hand and moved his fingers around the rim of his sunglasses with the intent of joking around. Unfortunately, he was met with a head nodding out of frustration.

"Dang," Chatwin said, walking toward Talia. When he got closer to her, he leaned forward to hear what she was saying.

"Take it slowly," she said to one of the ranch hands. "You're upsetting the horses."

"Yes, milady, we'll slow down."

"Thank you kindly," she replied. She brushed Spitfire's mane, and he calmed.

"Wow. That's Spitfire. I thought he didn't like anyone," Thomas remarked.

Chatwin smiled. "She has a way with animals, but you're right. We can't put him in the trailer. He doesn't play well with others. Thanks for the information." Chatwin started walking toward the trailers and yelled over his shoulder at Thomas. "Your check is already in the mail. You should get it today."

Thomas waved as he walked off.

"Hey! Everybody, listen up. Herman will take Spitfire in his trailer."

Seeing Chatwin, Talia smiled and said, "Is Herman's Hermit here?" She laughed at herself for giving him that nickname.

Chatwin nodded to the driveway. "He just pulled up."

"Oh, good. I'll take him, then," Talia said, linking her arm through his. "Would you like to walk with us to Herman's trailer?"

Yes, he thought. *I'd go with you anywhere.* But he knew he needed to distance himself from her. *Don't let yourself get in too deep,* he scolded himself. "We have a lot of packing to do," he said, unlinking his arm from hers.

"Yes, Your Highness," Talia said with a chuckle as she led Spitfire toward the trailer.

Chatwin watched her as she walked away. Then, a ranch hand approached him. "Sir, we have all the horses loaded. Tomorrow, we'll round up the rest of the cattle, goats, and sheep. We have an envoy heading our way early in the morrow."

"I don't know what I ever would have done without all my staff. I am so blessed. All of your hard work will be rewarded."

"Sir, we do not need a reward. You already pay us much more than any other estate workers. Working for you is an honor, and we would do anything for you, Sir. And if I must say, without your temper boiling..."

Chatwin gave him a 'watch it' look.

"Miss Talia brings happiness to you. We all see it. Your face glows when she is around, Sir."

"Well, she will be leaving soon, so get that out of your mind."

"Yes, sir." The ranch hand turned and went back to his task.

Chapter Twenty-Five

Inside the manor, the staff were busy packing boxes. Over the rustling of packing, Chatwin heard a popping sound, so he peeked around the corner and saw Talia popping bubble wrap. With each pop, she giggled like a little child. He smiled fondly and snuck up to his room without her knowing he was there.

Later that day, Bertie approached Chatwin's bedroom door, and just before he knocked, he heard Chatwin yelling. "There is no room for mistakes. I pay you dearly for results. There is no compromise for my guest's sake. I want this corrected immediately. I expect a call from you within the hour!"

The loud clang of the phone shuddered through the walls, and then Bertie heard the phone hit the floor. Bertie backed away from the door, deciding to speak to Chatwin later. Instead, he went and found Poppy.

"Poopy, my dear. Do you have a moment to talk?"

Her eyes twinkled. "You realize this is about the fourth or fifth time you called me Poopy, dear, sweet Bertie."

A smile formed on his face, but his eyes were heavy. "I thought you liked it."

"You're right. I do. I find it endearing."

"And that is my intention. At first, it was a whimsical mistake, but after repeating it a few times, it felt right. Sweet. Intimate. By now, we both are aware of our intimate feelings for each other."

Poppy blushed, and she pinched her lips together with a smile.

"Anyway, the good sir is in a tizzy, so we must ensure no one bothers him. As you know, that temper of his is hit or miss. It seems that only Talia can soften his raging temper, and yet he still terrifies her, at times. You know the dreaded date is coming quickly—the day when he will once again turn into a beast. If only..."

"If only we could find a way to avoid it?" Poppy responded. "I was hoping the business of packing and moving would distract him. As good as he is to us, his temper outbursts make me want to leave sometimes. I have never seen a man act so hopeless over a wife's death. He can't seem to get over it."

Bertie nodded.

"When the date comes around, I fear Talia will be in danger. After all, she is imprisoned because of it. Do you think he would actually hurt her? I mean, physically lay a hand on her? She has the courage of a warrior, and I am afraid she may rise up against him one day."

"We mustn't think about it," Bertie said. "Let's keep packing so we can get out of this place. Maybe we can move out on that terrible day and keep his mind preoccupied. I do love that man. He is like my own son. I adore him, but I fear for the lass."

"Aye. Me too," Poppy replied.

"Poppy, I told you before that I believe there is more to the story. He and Lily were truly in love. It was a beautiful thing. But, in my heart, I know there is more to it, but he won't confide in me. I can't figure out why he would hold something so important inside. What secret can turn the best man I know into a raging beast?"

She squeezed his hand, and her tender eyes watered for the hopeless situation.

~

At dinner time, the dining table hosted a feast fit for King Henry's knights. The table was set with platters of fish and chips, and old ale filled the men's glasses. All the staff had entered the dining room, but Talia noticed that Chatwin's chair remained vacant. She wondered if he was in a foul mood.

"What a fabulous surprise. Why old ale? We always get pop or water," Jonesy asked curiously.

"Why all the questions? Just eat and get back to work," Charles replied scathingly.

"The good sir wanted us all to have a good meal to keep up our strength from the extra workload. That is all," Poppy added.

The ringing of the buzzer caused several members of the staff to jump. Bertie walked into the kitchen to answer. "Yes, your Lordship?"

"Bertie, I have a lot of phone calls and paperwork I have to attend to. Please have my meal brought to my room."

"As you wish, sir."

Talia watched as Bertie climbed the stairs with the good sir's meal.

Oh well. I was looking forward to seeing him today, but I might as well enjoy this meal, Talia thought. She tried to take a bite, but her stomach rolled. "Charles, as yummy as this is, I just have no appetite. I'll save it for supper." She screeched her chair back and stood, grasping her plate.

With a puckered mouth and narrow eyes, Charles grabbed the plate from her hands and huffed his way into the kitchen.

Talia shook her head and gave everyone a grin, "I think I'll retire to my room."

In her room, she played a CD from a music group called For King and Country. She had never heard of them before. When they played the song "God Only Knows," she sat back on the bed and listened to the lyrics, feeling melancholy. Sorrowful tears dripped down her face. She thought of her years in imprisonment, and she wondered what her parents, the house staff, and her friends were doing.

Mrs. Pentagran came to her mind—with her sweet, wrinkled face, her weak hands, and her fragile body. *I wonder if she is still alive. Is anyone helping her with the cats or keeping her company? She was so full of wisdom and had such a pleasant outlook on life. I miss her.*

She envisioned her friends lying on the bed, twirling hair in their fingers, laughing and gossiping about that snobby Tulia. "My, she was a snotface." *I wonder what Chatwin is up to. I wonder if he got married,* she thought.

She smiled as she recollected their childhood adventures, thrashing through the brambles and ivy and throwing mud pies at each other. She thought about her Mum's face when she came home covered in mud. "That is not a very proper way for a young lass to act," her mum said.

She and Chatwin were always rescuing an injured animal. Talia and Chatwin would lie on the ground and watch when the staff set the wildlife free after they had nursed the animals back to health.

I swear Chatwin almost kissed me one time. He got so flustered. His face turned bright red, and he stuttered as he took off running. He was so cute.

CRASH! SWOOSH! A wave crashed against Talia's window, and she fell to the floor in fear. She got up, ran down the stairs, and nearly collided with Poppy.

Just then, Chatwin appeared. "What was that noise?"

Talia ran up and wrapped her arms around him, trembling. "Oh, sir. A huge wave crashed against my window. It scared the living daylights out of me. Tidbit! I forgot to check on him and his family." She turned around quickly and fled up the stairs to her room.

Chatwin followed, gripping his hands tightly in worry.

Walking in, he stumbled over some boxes and stopped, watching Talia hold Tidbit.

She turned her head toward him. "Oh, sir, he is just fine. They are all fine."

"What a relief. If you would like, we could move all of them to a huge carrier and take them into the den. I could have Poppy set it up for you to sleep there also, if you like."

"That would be wonderful. My body is still shaking with fear. Why does the sea hate us so? Why can't she be satisfied with what she has? No, she wants everything, including what belongs to us. I mean, you, sir."

Chatwin put his index finger to his mouth. *She feels like this is her home now. I am perplexed. This has to stop. She is invading my heart, softening it, faster and faster each day*. He gathered his composure. "I will go and have the carrier brought into the den and speak with Poppy."

Chapter Twenty-Six

Talia stretched her arms and yawned. The bright sun rays shone through the window, and she blinked her eyes to adjust to the light. When her vision cleared, she saw the good sir sitting by the mice cage. He was rubbing Tidbit's fur.

Suddenly, she heard a noise that sounded like a vacuum cleaner sucking in a watermelon. A member of the livestock staff was snoring. Talia chuckled.

Seeing that Talia was awake, Chatwin whispered, "Good morning, Lass."

Talia quietly unzipped her sleeping bag and slowly rose. Bertie snorted as he repositioned himself in his sleeping bag. Talia gently climbed over one body after the other to get to Chatwin.

When she reached him, she touched his shoulder and smiled sweetly. "Good morning to you, Sir."

Charles clanked a pan with a metal spoon to wake everyone.

"I could strangle him," Chatwin spewed. He stood and walked toward the kitchen. Talia and Poppy followed quietly. They snuck in the other entrance.

Chatwin was standing next to the stove with fiery eyes

glaring at Charles, who was wiping a dish with a tea towel. "What is the meaning of all that clanging, Charles?"

"Just alerting everyone for breakfast, Sir," Charles replied boldly.

Chatwin's eyes scanned the food sitting on the kitchen island. "What kind of mush is this?" You made this? Sick. It looks like vomit."

Charles' eyes were as wide as he could make them. His lips curved downward.

Talia let out a giggle. "Look, Poppy." She pointed to Chatwin. He glanced over at her, his brows drawn together. Poppy laughed gleefully.

"What is so amusing?" Chatwin asked.

"It's just… it's just that the steam from the teapot looks like it's coming out of your head, like you're steaming mad," Talia said as a chortle escaped her mouth.

He turned and looked directly at the teapot steaming. He realized how funny it must have looked and broke out into a guffaw.

Charles placed his hands on his hips and lifted his head. "There is nothing funny about criticizing me. Besides, this is all the food left in the house."

"On that note, Poppy, please inform the whole staff that I will be taking you out to breakfast. You, too, Charles," Chatwin said.

"Fine by me," Charles commented haughtily, his nose up in the air.

"We shall leave in twenty minutes. Let's get to it," Chatwin ordered.

～

"Oh, sir, this place is chockablock with people," Bertie said worriedly as they entered the diner.

"Let me handle this," Chatwin replied.

The cooks and waitresses had stopped what they were doing, staring at them. There weren't enough tables to sit everyone, and they obviously didn't have enough help.

Chatwin walked up to the counter. "Please don't fret. We are not in a hurry and can wait to be seated. Why, we'll even help set up the tables and make tea or coffee."

"But sir, regulations prohibit help from someone not employed here. You know, Health and Safety Executive rules and Employers Liability Insurance prohibits such things. You know, all that jolly, good stuff."

"Of course. You are correct. Well, can I pay you whatever it would cost to close the diner for a few hours?"

"Um... let me check with my manager. I'll be right back."

A few minutes later, an older woman entered the dining room, turned the "closed" sign on the door, and locked it.

"We're good to go," Chatwin yelled.

An hour and a half later, they were all sitting around tables, filling their bellies.

"Sir, I had the strangest dream," Talia told Chatwin. "It felt so real, and I remember every vivid detail about it."

"Let's hear it. Must have been quite the dream by looking at the expression on your face."

"It was, Sir. I actually feel like I was there. There was this cute girl with a hair color that's hard to describe. It was kind of a green-gray mixture, which sounds hideous, but on her, it was beautiful. She was running toward me as fast as she could with fear in her eyes. I looked past her and saw a man chasing her. I couldn't breathe. Tears fell like a waterfall down her face. Then she rubbed her eyes, and it looked like the sun burst out of them. When she ran past me, I saw bright red marks around her neck as though she had been choked. And the last thing I heard was her name being yelled from this rotten man chasing her. 'Galaxas! Galaxas, come back!' Then, something flew past me silently, but it was so fast, I couldn't make out what it was, and when I looked around for the girl, she had disappeared—

vanished like a ghost. Oh, and when that thing passed by, a dandelion dropped to the ground."

"How intriguing and how crazy that you remember all the details. I wonder if it means anything," Chatwin said.

"I only know that I was intrigued, scared, amazed, and terrified. I can still see her face. I had this strange suspicion that she was intelligent, sweet as candy, and creative as a world-renowned artist. Even stranger, something inside my head kept alerting me to her importance, as though she were royalty from some unknown world. How cuckoo is that?"

"If you ask me, I find it absolutely fascinating," Chatwin said.

"Excuse me, sir, but is there anything else I can get fer you?" the waitress asked Chatwin.

"Hold on, please. Does anyone need anything else?" he yelled, pushing himself up from the chair.

"No, thank you," staff members rang out.

"I think we are good to go, Miss."

While the good sir took care of the bill, Talia stood beside the window, deep in thought. The older waitress walked up and put her arm around her shoulder. "Follow your heart, even if love takes you to the stars in the heavens or down into the depths of the sea. Reach high, little one. Reach high."

Talia's mouth dropped. *Why did she say that to me? That was the very same thing Poppy told me. Are you trying to tell me something, Lord?*

❧

Back at home, Chatwin briefly explained what needed to be done.

"Sir, could we take a stroll around the premises before you head up to your room and pack? Pretty please," Talia asked him.

"Well, fortunately for you, I just have a small amount of packing left, so sure. Let's do it."

She wrapped her arm around his as they walked. She tugged on a branch of Adams Laburnum and inhaled its sweet, woodsy fragrance, which reminded her of violas. The cluster of flowers was always show-stopping, but a resident of the UK would have to wait until June or July to see the blooms.

"What a devastation it will be to have that monstrous sea destroy this beauty," Talia said with weary eyes.

"I tend to agree, Lass. It is criminal. Simply criminal."

They walked in silence, her hand resting on his arm.

"Dirty scoundrel!" Chatwin yelled suddenly.

"What is it you are speaking of, sir?"

"Listen. Do you hear the sea? No, of course not, because it defeated me. It no longer has to roar and battle me. Shhh, listen. Do you hear its laughter? It mocks me."

She looked up at him, worried. "Sir, I fear your mind is headed down the wrong path. You must be imagining whatever it is you're hearing. You're sounding like a nutter. Possibly you need sleep?"

He looked down at her, and an affectionate smile formed. "Wipe that fearful look off your face, Lass. I'm kidding. But isn't it odd that the sea is at peace with itself since we will be completely moved out tomorrow?"

"If ye put it that way, Sir, then, yes, it is odd indeed."

Chapter Twenty-Seven

Back in the manor, Talia watched Chatwin walk up the stairs to his room. She thought about when she secretly searched his room for clues to prove that he was a vampire, werewolf, or monster. Of course, she found nothing, and surprisingly, now, she looked at him with fondness.

Poppy watched Talia from across the room with a look of concern. Seeing Poppy's face, Talia asked, "What is it?"

"Could we talk in the den, please?"

Talia placed her arm in Poppy's as they walked to the den. "You're giving me a fright, Poppy."

"Oh, Lass. Bertie came to me moments ago and pulled me aside. We have managed to keep our Lordship preoccupied with the move, but tomorrow's date is traumatic for him. That's why he is sending us on this cruise. You haven't seen anything as terrifying as his rage on this particular date. Bertie fears when he packs the sentimental items he has kept hidden out of his sight, it will bring out the beast in him. It never fails. Each year during this time, it happens. I stayed hidden for days. Actually, mostly only Bertie deals with him. You see, our Lordship hired me years ago to prepare for your arrival. That was my sole purpose here. If he wasn't able to find you, then he said he would find me employment elsewhere."

"Wait! He was looking for me? He didn't just stumble upon me in the forest? Why? Why was he looking for me?"

Poppy dropped her head. "I have said too much. I don't know why I was blabbering on. I guess I'm just nervous. You must forget what you heard. Do not ask him about it. I beg of you. He'd be furious, and you may think you've seen his anger, but trust me, you haven't. After some of his rants, we had to hire a contractor to repair all the damage done to the house."

Talia's head and shoulders slumped. "For your sake, Poppy, I will not say a word."

"Good. Also, I think it best if you remain out of sight."

Talia's face wrinkled. "How? Where? Why?"

"Just beware and be prepared to flee from his sight. That is all."

Chatwin was nearly packed when he found a floral-designed box. Her scent still lingered on it. He closed his eyes, brought the box to his nose, and sniffed. She came right into his thoughts. With trembling hands, he grabbed the trinkets and rubbed them. Shaking, he grabbed the wedding ring, kissed it, and closed his eyes to remember their wedding day. Tears dribbled down his cheek.

He picked up a stack of letters held together with a beautiful ribbon. He brought the stack to his nose and sniffed her still-lingering fragrance. He untied the ribbon with wobbly fingers. After reading each love letter, he set them aside, sighing heavily as sobs shook his body.

Then, he picked up a photo. He smiled as he rubbed her face, then collapsed onto the bed, holding her photo. With another violent outburst of sobs, he gasped for air and rolled into a ball, holding the photo to his heart, drawing his knees up, and squeezing the photo with all his might.

Suddenly, it felt like something brushed up against him. It was soft like a feather. He sat up on the bed, wiping the stormy tears from his face. He looked around, but the room was empty. Next, he stood up and walked around the room, but no one was there.

This was why he kept to himself most of the time—so he wouldn't feel the pain of losing anyone else near and dear to his heart. He knew he might as well be a vampire because his heart was as hard as a rock. But that's the way he wanted it. He never wanted to feel this pain again.

He walked back to the box lying on his bed. The memories are bittersweet, but he had to look at them like he did year after year. Didn't he owe his wife that much?

The next photo he grabbed was of his parents and his wife. It was Christmas Eve.

Their last Christmas Eve together. His stomach churned, and his eyes filled with bittersweet tears.

"Look how happy we were. My parents loved Lily as if she were their very own daughter. And she loved them," he whispered.

Then, he picked up the photograph of him with Lily and her parents. "They loved me like I was their own son, too, and I abandoned them all."

His hand shook as he picked up the picture of him and Lily. He laid the photo back down and squeezed his hands tightly to stop the trembling. Then he picked the picture back up and cuddled the photo under his chin as he sobbed.

He fell onto the bed, gripping the comforter like a lifeline. *Why? Why does this haunt me so? Will it always be this way? God, help me?*

"But You, Lord, have abandoned me. Ye laugh at my loneliness. Is this a game to You? A test, like Job? How could You take away the people in my life whom I have loved with my whole heart? How could You? Now, look at what I have become. And how could You allow that monster to live, to be free from any criminal charges? He walks free? It is not I who is a monster, Lord. Oh, no. It is he. Taking something from me that I loved with my whole heart and, in return, taking something from him that he loves with all his heart is absolute justice, and You know it."

His thoughts went to the funeral. Lilies were abundant because she was named after them, a symbol of innocence. Members of the private gathering were forbidden to wear black, the customary color of clothing for a funeral. They were requested to wear blue, her favorite color.

After he disappeared, he didn't keep in touch with anybody. When he finally called home, Bertie answered and informed him that his parents had passed away, both with a heart condition.

They died of a broken heart. "I broke their heart, and they died because of me." He stood and gripped his hair in his hands and pulled with anger.

Pacing back and forth, he yelled, "I should just end it. This will never change. The torment will never stop. I should just go throw myself into that devilish sea. You win! You win, Satan!"

~

Hearing the good sir's roars, Talia ran into Poppy's arms. Her body trembled with fear in Poppy's embrace. Poppy moved her hands up and down Talia's arms, trying to comfort her, but she was shaking, too.

Poppy pulled Talia's chin up and looked into her frightened eyes. "Why don't you go outside and walk around the estate... just in case, Lass."

"That's a good idea. I will do that. Why don't you come with me? You must be scared, yourself."

"If things get treacherous, I will come out and find you. I'm going to stick around and see what happens first."

Chapter Twenty-Eight

Still pacing, Chatwin passed the window and froze.

Talia was facing his direction, running her fingers down a weeping willow's limb. The wind blew her shimmering hair, and pieces of her clothes' soft, white fabric flapped in the gusts. The sun shone down on her, and dewdrops glistened on the ground around her. It was absolutely magnificent to witness.

He watched her, astonished. "It's an angel. She's really an angel. She takes my breath away. Could I have *real* feelings for her? Could I love her? That's preposterous. I'm forcing these thoughts so I don't have to face the reality that I can never love again. True love only exists once in a lifetime. Anything after that is a substitute. Talia deserves to find true love, but she'll not be able to get that from me."

In defeat, he sat back down on the bed and picked up another photo, and instantly, he was catapulted into the past.

It was the day before New Year's Eve. He and Lily planned to take a romantic weekend trip together. They both were excited and had been packing for days. He had a meeting in the morning, and she had a doctor's appointment around the same time, so they drove together.

"What's in that box in the backseat?" he asked her.

"Oh, just a box I meant to take out of the car yesterday. That is all." She smiled sweetly.

"Well, then, I'll see you in about two hours," Chatwin said as he kissed her sweet, delectable lips and jumped out of the car.

"I'll pick you up in a couple hours," she said, and she blew him a kiss as she drove away.

Later that day, Chatwin was leaning on a lamppost when he saw his wife pull up to the stoplight. He stood tall and waved at her, smiling. She smiled at him and blew him another kiss. When the light turned green, she moved forward.

Then, he watched as a car slammed into the corner of his wife's car. Her vehicle fishtailed and smashed into a lamppost. The crash was so loud. How can anything be that loud? It sounded like buildings tumbled onto the car. As the blood drained from his face, he stood motionless. He couldn't think clearly, thinking he was imagining it all. When he finally got his wits about him, he ran, screaming her name. "Lily! Lily, I'm coming."

Tears dripped down his face as he ran. Cars screeched and honked as he ran into traffic. He only focused on her car.

What car? It was nothing but a tangled mess. As he approached, the vehicle that hit Lilly's car pulled away. Chatwin froze, and as the vehicle passed him, he saw the man's face through the window.

When the fire brigade rolled in, everyone moved out of the way except for Chatwin, who was still trying to open the car door. "Lily, I can't... I can't... I can't get the door open."

"Sir, please step back. We will get her out," the firefighter said in haste.

The Jaws of Life cut through the metal, sparks spitting in the air. The grinding sound made Chatwin cover his ears. Finally, the firefighters gently pulled her from the car. She groaned in pain. They laid her on the ground, waiting for the stretcher.

Chatwin pulled her head onto his lap, holding her hand. "You're going to be okay. Please, be okay," he slobbered out.

She smiled up at him and slowly, with much difficulty, put her hand on his face. "I love..." Her hand fell over his.

He shook her gently. "Lily. Lily! Don't go. Please don't go. Please..."

He couldn't finish his sentence, but he stared at her, stroking her hair, unaware of her broken bones and the puddle of blood forming underneath them.

People stood around bawling their eyes out, and the air lingered with anguish.

The medics helped him up, and one held his limp body as they took her away. He was an empty shell. Then, another medic walked up and handed him the box that was in the backseat, but he was still unresponsive.

That evening, he sat in his parents' bedroom and opened the box. He let out a roaring scream that echoed throughout the house. His parents rushed into the room and looked inside the box. They couldn't console him; they needed consoling themselves.

Chatwin was adamant that his parents not tell a living soul of the contents in the box. He would never be able to discuss it again.

After that night, he committed himself to an institution for therapy, but nothing could snap him out of it. That was when he decided to disappear. He was hurting his parents, and it just wasn't right. He hid for a year.

Then, one day, he snapped out of it, and the remembrance of what happened came back to him. He called home to find out his parents had passed away. Then, he took over the business and worked day and night to make a more-than-profitable portfolio. The staff was moved to their new location, and he spent endless years planning how to get even. That was where Talia came into the picture—to ensure her father would live with the emptiness and pain he could never get over.

Chatwin threw everything back into the keepsake box and tossed it into a packing box. He roared, spitting out profanity. The chairs he threw crashed into the wall and broke into pieces. The wood hitting the floor clanked as it rumbled to a stop.

Talia looked up to see shards of glass shatter to the ground as a chair flew through the window, hitting the ground outside with a thud and bursting into pieces. She ran back to the house and saw the staff huddled together in a circle close to the stairway to his chambers. She ran to them, and they all embraced her—even Charles.

The staff listened to a tearing sound that seemed to rip forever.

In his room, the stuffing from the comforter floated around the room. His punches to the wall sounded like an excavator dropping its bucket onto the ground. His knuckles bled, but he continued hitting the wall as if he felt no pain.

"This time of year, has always been unpleasant, but I have never witnessed this fury.

I fear the man is possessed," Bertie whispered.

The hurling of his door flying open caused them to jump, and they tightened their arms around Talia.

~

Chatwin hated himself for allowing Talia to weaken the hate he had built up over the years.

I betrayed myself, my wife, and my parents. I betrayed true love itself. No, I don't love her. Talia is just a distraction. If I truly loved her, then why would my memories betray me so? Why do they torment me so wickedly? It is all useless. Death is the only solution to take away the torment.

Heavy and fast stomps thundered through the house as he ran down the stairs. He saw Talia and the staff huddled together. *Pathetic weaklings.* "Why are you still here?" he roared.

"We'll leave now, good sir."

"Good sir? You have to be kidding? There is nothing good about me!" he roared louder.

"Come, everyone. Grab your suitcases. We're going now. Go on, now," Bertie urged them.

"Hold on," Chatwin yelled. "Drop *her* off at a tower block. I never want to see the likes of her ever again. EVER!"

Poppy tried pulling Talia away, but she stood frozen—speechless. Fear, anger, and hurt washed over her face. The hate and contempt in his eyes caused her to shiver. *He hates me. He really hates me. But why? What changed? What did I do?*

She teared up, but her rage emerged. "What have I done to you, *Sir*, to bring out so much contempt? I thought we had feelings for each other. You seemed to enjoy my company. I was beginning to feel like I was living in a fairy tale come true, not even wanting my freedom."

"Fairy tales aren't real, silly girl."

"I am not some silly girl, you vile beast. Fairy tales *do* exist. Are you familiar with *Beauty and the Beast?*"

"Talia, just come on." Poppy tried pulling her away. Talia withdrew her hand and yelled, "No. I want to know what I have ever done to you. Why do you torment a staff who serves you and treats you with the utmost respect and love? How dare you repay them with such vileness."

"Shut your gob!" Chatwin shouted at her.

"No, I won't shut my mouth. You shut *your* mouth!"

He huffed loudly.

"Is it a virgin sacrifice that you want? Will that save these dear, sweet people from your wrath, Beast? If that is what it takes, then here. Take me, you bloodthirsty swine." She spat at him.

Bertie stepped up to Talia and grabbed her hand. "Please, Miss Talia. Come with me."

She pulled her hand away and puffed out her chest. To the good sir, she yelled, "Why do you hate me so? I want an answer."

"It isn't *you* I hate. It's who you represent. Your..."

"My what? How can I appease you if I don't know what you're talking about?"

"I don't want your appeasement. I don't want you. I don't need anyone. You, my staff, your God. No one!"

"You're wrong, Sir," Talia said, her voice lower now. "You *do* need your staff, and you *do* need me, and most of all, you need my God." She shook her head and smirked at him. "You, sir, are not a man. You are most certainly a beast possessed by Satan himself. I fear I may be looking right into the eyes of the Prince of Darkness."

Chatwin had forgotten to disguise himself, not that it mattered. His long, scraggly beard and hair hung down to his shoulders in clumps, and his eyes seared with contempt. His upper body rose up and down with loud, ragged breaths. He stepped toward her with his hands clutched, ready to grab her. His mouth was opened, exposing his teeth.

His fiery eyes now terrified her, and his massive hands trembled as he moved closer to her. He clutched his fingers tightly as if he could feel her neck in his hands.

Bertie yelled frantically, "My Lordship, stop. I beg you. Stop!"

Talia screamed, turned, and ran outside toward the front gate. A torrential storm had come, but the scene inside was too ominous for anyone to notice. His footsteps thudded behind her, and she ran faster, panting for breath.

"Stop," Chatwin yelled. "Talia, don't touch the gate. Stop! Please!" *No, God,* he prayed. *She doesn't deserve to die, not like this.*

Just as her hand reached for the gate, he caught her. Being so close to the gate, shockwaves zapped through her body, and she tumbled to the ground. He caught her before she fell into the gate.

Lightning shot throughout the sky, with thunder pounding like bombs exploding, and Chatwin thought Talia was dead as he carried her lifeless body back to the manor.

On the front portico, he gently placed her on the ground and shook her shoulders. "Talia, wake up. Please. Talia. Talia. Talia." Lightning lit up the sky around him.

The staff stood at the door, holding each other, crying.

Without looking up, Chatwin yelled, "Bertie, Poppy, help. Help her. Get someone to start the chopper. Call and have an ambulance meet us at the usual spot. Hurry!"

At this point, they felt hate for him, but for Talia's sake, they moved quickly.

Chatwin was determined to ride in the helicopter with her, but there wasn't enough room, and Bertie had the hardest time removing him so the medic helicopter could take off.

When they returned home, they exited Chatwin's chopper and walked to the castle. The rain was soft, now sounding like a mild shower, but the pain in Chatwin's heart felt like tornadic whirl-winds. Bertie refused to look at Chatwin. Poppy stood in the doorway, her eyes red from crying, her body trembling.

Bertie embraced her in a silent hug.

Like a shout of victory, the sea crashed over the cliff, tearing down the cliff's wall.

Chatwin glanced at the crumbling wall, and he fell to the ground and shook with sobs. Tears gushed out of his eyes. Heaves of anguish rocked his body.

"He isn't the man I swore to uphold," Bertie told Poppy. "He is nothing but a beast. Satan himself. I can no longer swear my loyalty to a man who no longer exists."

"Nor I," Poppy responded with sadness.

Bertie sternly called out to him, "You asked me how anyone could sparkle the way she does. I'll tell you why. She was sent from God above. Her love is the dew from heaven. The way she loves so completely, you can't find a stronger love than that, except for what the gracious Lord did Himself for mankind. You are a monster, sir—an absolute monster."

"Bertie, please, don't leave me. Poppy, please don't leave me," he begged, his voice strained. "I am so sorry. I will change. I Promise." Before Bertie could respond, Chatwin moaned in torment and continued. "You don't know everything, Bertie. It's too painful to speak of. Too much pain. I love Talia. I couldn't bear to admit it, but it's the truth. How can I betray Lily? But I love her—I truly love Talia—so much so that it angered me. You don't know everything, Bertie. You don't know."

Chatwin fell face down in the rain.

Bertie stared, amazed at the sparkling dew all around Chatwin. It was usually only visible around Talia. He nudged Poppy. "Am I hallucinating?"

Her mouth opened in wonderment. "No. I see it, too."

"We can't abandon him," Bertie said, staring at Poppy. She nodded, and hand in hand, they ran to Chatwin.

When they reached him, Chatwin was unconscious, lying in the mud.

"We have to get him inside. Go get some help," Bertie told Poppy.

Still unconscious, Chatwin lay silently on the guest room bed. When Poppy entered, she saw that Bertie was still sitting beside the bed.

"What did the doctor say?" Poppy asked.

"He'll be okay. He said that our lordship has endured extreme stress and that his body is forcing him to rest—to convalesce."

Bertie rose and removed a razor from the drawer.

"What are you doing?" Poppy asked.

"We're done with this charade," he said as he slopped shaving cream all over Chatwin's face. After one swipe, he held the razor out to Poppy. She covered her mouth, and her eyes widened. After a few more swipes, she removed her hands, and her face lit up.

After using a towel to wipe Chatwin's face clean, Bertie cut his hair.

"Oh, my goodness," Poppy said, covering her face. "He's not a beast at all."

Chapter Twenty-Nine

The next morning, Chatwin opened and closed his eyes several times to adjust to the light. He looked around and saw that the room was filled with flowers and balloons. "Am I dead? I can't be in heaven. Bertie, are you here?"

Bertie sat on the bed and pulled him into an embrace. "I'm here, your Lordship. I won't leave you."

Tears trickled down both of their faces.

"Poppy! Did she leave me?" Chatwin asked.

"No, your Lordship. I shall not leave you either," Poppy said, grasping his hand.

"Obviously, I'm not dead because I don't feel the heat of flames."

"No, good sir, you're home, where you belong," Bertie answered.

Chatwin's hand moved to stroke his beard, but it wasn't there. His eyes bulged. He felt around his face and then his hair, looking at Bertie with fright.

"Here, Sir. Take a look." Bertie held up a mirror. "I forgot what a dashing, handsome man you are."

"Wow! Frankly, so did I. I can't believe this is me." He was silent momentarily, and then shock registered on his face. "Talia! Please tell me she is alive," he said, sitting up abruptly.

"Easy, sir. Easy," Bertie said, attempting to push him back onto the bed. "Talia is alive and doing well."

"Then, why do you have a look of sadness?"

"It's just that we have waited so long for you to accept the love of that angel, and hearing the concern in your voice melts our hearts."

"I love her, Bertie." He looked at Poppy. "I love her."

"We know, sir," Poppy said. "I've known for some time."

"I've always known," Bertie added.

"Where is she? Is she still in the hospital?" Chatwin asked.

"Aye. The doctor said she passed out from stress. He also said that feeling the electric waves from the gate added to her stress. And no. We did not tell the doctor about you. So, everything in that regard is fine," Bertie exclaimed.

"Flowers. We need to fill her room with flowers. Would you mind calling the florist?"

"No, your Lordship. She likes wildflowers," Bertie reminded him.

"Ah, yes. Then, hire as many people as you can to find some. Hurry, Bertie."

Bertie smiled. "I knew you would suggest it, so it's already done."

"You won't believe what I'm about to say, but she deserves her freedom. Please get ahold of her parents and send all her things to their house, including the critters. She could never live without them."

"I knew you would suggest that also. It's all done, Sir," Bertie said.

"You know, people search all over the world for hidden treasure, but I have it all. I always have." He grabbed Bertie and Poppy's hands and smiled with loving warmth. "I've been surrounded by angels my whole life but couldn't see it because of my pain. I see it now. I'm good to go," he whispered. He was so exhausted that his hands slipped to the bed, and he fell fast asleep.

"Ohhh!" Poppy screeched.

"He's fine, my dear. He just needs to sleep. Come on. We could use some of that, too."

Chapter Thirty

When Talia awoke the next morning, everything was a blur. She jumped up in her hospital bed, bracing her arms behind her, unaware of her surroundings.

"Talia, my darling daughter," her mum said through trickling tears.

"Mum, is that you?" Talia's hand touched her mother's face.

"Yes, Tal, it is your mum."

"Oh, Mum, I've missed you so much."

They embraced, both crying happy tears. Then Talia looked and saw a man sitting on a chair beside her. He didn't move or speak; he just sat there with tears running down his face.

"Father, is that you?"

He shook his head and sobbed. Talia pushed herself over to him, and they hugged. Eventually, she sat back, and her father gently touched her cheek as sentimental eyes looked into hers.

"I thought I'd never see you again," he said, fighting back tears.

"I thought the same thing, Father."

~

When she could speak without crying, Talia asked, "How did I get here?"

"All your things, including some mice, were mysteriously sitting on our doorstep. Then, we got an anonymous call from a gentleman who told us to come to the hospital. On the phone, he was quite affectionate in his tone concerning you. He told us that it was as though you came down from heaven to save a man from isolation and brought much-needed life and love to their house. Then, he told us that you are free to live your life in freedom. He said all this while choking up on his words, I may add.

"He didn't explain where you've been and why you've been away, and to be honest, we were so anxious to get to the hospital, we didn't even question him. Anyway, the doctor said you should be okay to go home tomorrow, and we can discuss it all," her mother explained. "I would like to know where you've been."

Tears fell down Talia's face again.

"My dear daughter, you don't seem happy to be home," Talia's father commented, frowning.

"You couldn't be more wrong, Father, but I came to love these people who cared for me. You would, too, but you're right; let's focus on our reunion for now. I have missed you all so much. Huh! What about Twiggly Wigglesbottom and Ms. Adelaide? Please tell me they are well."

"They are home preparing your room and caring for your critters upon your return."

She smiled brightly.

After her parents left, Talia sat back against some pillows and wrapped her arms around her knees, thinking. She tried to remember the argument—well, her battle with the "Lordship" or "Good Sir." Her face formed into a scowl, and her eyes teared up, remembering the vicious things he said to her. She rocked back and forth on the bed, lying her face on her arms to cry. *Why do I miss him so? I miss them all. Why am I not happier about being home? I am happy, but I miss them so much.*

A nurse walked into the room and checked Talia's vitals. Talia was in no mood to speak, so she just listened to the bleep, bleep, bleep of the annoying monitor.

"Pfff." She didn't mean to sigh so loudly.

"Are you okay, dear? The doctor believes any memory impairment will be normal in a week or two," the kind nurse added.

"Memory impairment? My memory is just fine. I hate being confined like this, but I hear I will be released tomorrow. How long have I been here, anyway?"

"About three days."

"I have been unconscious all that time?"

"Yes, but your vitals have been good," the nurse added. "A man flew you in a helicopter to meet the medic chopper, but he was so distressed over you that he kept crying, making it difficult to find out necessary details. He even put up a fight when the medics said it was too dangerous for him to be in the 'copter,' that it would be too many people and too heavy. He was really upset about your condition. He must really love you."

Her eyes shot wide open, and her mouth dropped. At first, she couldn't speak; then, without moving or looking at the nurse, she mouthed the words, "He was upset and didn't want to leave me?"

"The medics said it was turning into an actual punch-up, but when they told him it would be too dangerous to have so many people in the copter and that you needed immediate attention, he came to his senses and apologized. He held a thumb up and said to them, 'Good to go.'"

Talia smiled at that statement.

"They said they had never seen a man so emotional like he was out of his mind. I was the nurse who helped get you out of the copter, and they told me this as we hurried to get you into the examination room."

Talia took it all in. Goosebumps developed on her skin, and she felt alive.

"Also, they said this man looked like he came out of the wilderness—said nobody could identify him if they tried; he was covered up with so much hair, like a Neanderthal or something. What gives with that?"

She didn't know how to respond, so she said, "That's because he *did* come out of the wilderness to rescue me." She remembered the first time she met him in the wilderness and how he saved her from being raped.

The nurse looked quizzically at her but decided to leave it alone and urged Talia to get some sleep.

I knew it. I knew he cared about me, and I felt he may have been in love with me. I wonder. Talia curled up on the bed and fell to sleep with a smile.

Chapter Thirty-One

W hat a celebration the household had with Talia at home again. Word spread throughout the region, and all her friends stopped over. Day after day and week after week, she had visitors daily. During that time, she explained what happened to her, beginning with the first abduction. Her father listened with much intensity. Talia described her time with the good sir, Bertie, Poppy, and the rest of the household but tried to conceal as much as possible to protect them.

"Father, forgive me so, but are you well? You have lost so much weight." Talia stared at his fragile body.

"I have health issues, but nothing to worry about, my sweet child. Please don't worry."

$\sim$

After a while, Talia engaged in normal activities and even enrolled in more uni courses, but she didn't realize a sad countenance painted her face.

Twiggly pulled her aside one day. He sat her down, gently gripped her arms, and looked deeply into her eyes. "Talk to me,

Tal. Did bad things happen to you? You need to speak with someone, maybe a therapist. I can't bear to watch you walk around in such a depression."

"What? I didn't even realize I was doing that. Oh, Twiggly, I love you all so much, and I am truly happy to be home again with all of you."

"Then, why won't you go hang out with your friends? In truth, dearie, you seem to be moping around. Talk to me."

"What can I say? As much as I love being here with all of you and missed you all every day I was gone, well, I also miss the staff who took such good care of me. We were family, too."

"Tell me about this 'good sir.'" His voice was sarcastic.

"There are so many aspects to his personality. He could be kind and witty—and frightening. He was quick to anger but also gentle, smart, and loyal."

"Sounds like Jekyll and Hyde."

"No! Well, yes, at times, but he was good to me. He cared for me, made me take college courses online, met any need I had, and even prepared a *Beauty and the Beast* ball just for me. It was magical, and he means a lot to me—they all do."

Twiggly watched her for a minute like he was trying to analyze what she had just said. Then, his face lit up. "Are you in love with this man?"

"That's preposterous, Twiggly. I spent all my teen years without any friends or boyfriends, so I don't even understand what a relationship is all about. I wouldn't know what being in love feels like. How could I?"

"Did he hurt you? I need to know the truth."

"No! No, Twiggly, and don't you dare give anyone the impression that he did. I care for him, and he took good care of me."

"Will you ever see him again?"

She dropped her head because she didn't want him to see her eyes tearing up. "I don't know."

Twiggly cupped her chin in his hand, and tears trickled down her cheeks even though she refused to open her eyes. "This, little one, is what it feels like to be in love."

Talia opened her eyes and stared into space. "How do you know that? Have you ever been in love?"

"Well, as a matter of fact, yes, and I just bought a ring and plan to propose. Shhh, it's a secret."

"Oh Twiggly." She jumped into his arms. "I couldn't be happier if I tried. Who, Twiggly? Who is she?"

"Someone you love very much."

Just then, Adelaide walked into the room. "There you two are. What are you two up to?" Her hands, balled into fists, went to her hips.

Twiggly and Talia looked at each other and laughed.

"Not a thing, my dear. Not a thing," Twiggly answered with a big smile.

Chapter Thirty-Two

After a restless night's sleep, Talia paced in her room, staring out the window, but being so deep in thought, she was not able to see the beautiful blooms of the primrose, bulbous buttercup, and goat's beard in the meadow outside of the backyard. As a child, she picked handfuls daily and laid in them as she daydreamed. But thoughts were consuming, and all she could think about was him. Her good sir. Her beast.

Why hasn't he checked up on me? What about Poppy and Bertie? We were family, too. "Lord above, please don't abandon me again. Sorry. You have never abandoned me. I just took my eyes off of You in my deep despair. Let me see them. I pray and beg of You, one last time, to say goodbye."

From under her bedroom door, a trail of Patti cakes aroma and homemade maple syrup swirled around her nose. No one needed to tell her it was brekkie time. After throwing a robe on, she merrily skipped down the stairs and danced into the kitchen.

She kissed Adelaide's cheek, hugged Twiggly, and twirled around like she was engaged in a folk dance before kissing her parents' cheeks.

"Good morning, all."

"It is so good to see you in a chipper mood this bright and happy morning," her mother commented with relief.

"How could I not be with these aromas floating around? It's downright despicable, I tell you. How could anyone, try as they may, be in a foul mood with such delectable aromas? You are a genius, Ms. Adelaide."

"It's about time someone noticed." Adelaide's chin raised proudly at the statement.

"After brekkie, I shall take Tidbit out to the meadow. Have you ever seen anything so lovely as those wildflowers?"

"I am well pleased to see you have noticed them once again, my daughter. It does my heart good." Talia's mother smiled.

"Adelaide, Twiggly, please join us for breakfast," Talia begged.

"Tal, we have been eating meals together ever since you disappeared. We may not be family by blood, but our bond is as strong as any family, dearest," Twiggly informed her.

As they ate, two butterflies floated past the window. Talia smiled and followed them with her eyes. She was turning back into her old self.

"Father, would it be all right for me to take a boat ride? You know how much I loved doing that as a child."

"If you must, but you will need supervision because I will not take any chances of you being abducted again. I have meetings, but maybe later."

Everyone was tied up with daily activities, so she let it drop.

"I almost forgot," Adelaide yelled enthusiastically. "At the market yesterday, there was talk around town about bustling activity at now Marquess Chatwin's estate. Remodeling, home improvement, a gorgeous landscape do-over, and much talk about some big corporations already doing business in our small town. Some will be building their business right here. People are ecstatic about the opportunities, and some are already benefiting from this good fortune. "Talk is that they believe

Marquess Chatwin has come home—or is coming home. No one has actually seen him, though. But they do think he is behind the prosperity coming our way."

"That is simply smashing," Twiggly commented with a happy smile.

"How exciting. I haven't seen him since childhood," Talia said. "Father, why aren't you more excited about this?"

"I'm sorry, dear, but I was interested in an article in the paper and wasn't paying much attention. I did hear some of the conversation, and yes, it is very good for our town." He patted Talia's knee and returned his focus to the paper.

Later, lying in the meadow with Tidbit, Talia closed her eyes and sniffed the fragrance of the wildflowers into her memory. She couldn't help but be excited to see her friend, Chatwin, and this was a great distraction to her lonely thoughts for the good sir.

Weeks went by when, one day, Adelaide ran into the house with the mail, holding up an invitation and grinning ear to ear. "Mrs. Brennyinn, where are you?" She yelled loudly enough to alert the neighbors next door.

"What is it, for gracious sakes?" Mrs. Brennyinn remarked in an annoyed voice.

"Look at this invitation. Look!"

By this time, Twiggly, Talia, and her father ran into the room to see what all the commotion was about. Freya's hand went to her mouth, and she sighed excitedly.

"Freya, I demand to know what is going on," Lord Brennyinn snapped.

Talia twisted her fingers with excitement.

Freya looked up from the invitation at each person. A big smile formed, and she announced, "The Marquess Chatwin

Kendrick Alexander Riley George requests all of our presence at the welcome home party for Talia and himself. He heard of Talia's return and insists on inviting the whole town for the reunion. It says so on this handwritten letter that he placed inside the invitation."

Talia hopped around like she was a child. Twiggly and Adelaide joined hands and twirled around the room.

"How generous to invite the help staff to such a huge event," Adelaide said.

Freya looked over at her husband, bothered by his lack of enthusiasm. "Really, Oliver, you could show a little excitement at the news of his return and this huge celebration."

"I'm sorry, dear. I guess I'm just shocked by hearing he has finally returned. What date is the party, by the way? I have several business trips scheduled."

"It is next Friday evening."

"As I suspected. I will be out of town, but please, you all enjoy yourselves and take lots of pictures."

"Oliver, this reunion includes your daughter's return. Can't you cancel this trip?"

"There is no way. It has been scheduled for months, and all the partners struggled to find a date that would suit all of us. I'm sorry, but it can't be changed."

Talia's eyes lowered, and her smile faded.

"Please understand I have no choice in the matter. It is time to build up our businesses. We have been struggling financially for a while."

"Father, I have noticed the house is rundown. What happened? Is that why you look so tired?"

"Maybe that does have something to do with it, but we'll be back on our feet in no time. Do not worry, little one. Then home improvements will be made."

Talia hugged her worried father. It broke her heart to see him struggling. "I understand, Father. I promise to take lots of pictures at the reunion."

When Talia walked into the kitchen to get some water, she saw Adelaide cleaning up some dishes.

"Ad, what happened to our finances?" Talia asked her. "Why is everything so run down, and where are the horses?"

"Child, I was given strict orders not to speak about it. I cannot betray your parents' confidence. Try Twiggly. He's much better at that sort of thing."

Talia snickered at the portrayal of gossipy Twiggly. She could always get him to talk.

Then she squeezed Adelaide's arm and strolled out of the kitchen, searching for Twiggly.

"There you are. Could I speak with you in private, Twig?'

"Of course, you may. Come this way so we are out of reach of anyone's hearing. I think some of our family members have heightened hearing senses."

She giggled.

"First, Twig, I promise I will not speak of this to anyone." Talia crossed her heart.

"Now, would you mind telling me what happened to our finances, and why everything is so rundown?"

Twiggly's fist covered his mouth, pushing up his nose as he thought. "Okay, but if you tell anyone, it will cause me to lose my job. Are we clear on this?"

"Absolutely. You know you can trust me. Does anyone besides me know of your plans to propose to Adelaide?" She raised an eyebrow at him.

"No, as a matter of fact. Just you know of my plans."

"There. See?"

"That's my girl. I can always trust you. Well then, let's get on with it. It is a short and sweet answer. When you were abducted, your father sold the horses, family goods, and most of the savings to search for you. He would never give up looking. We were all in agreement. Sometimes, the only pay for our services was to have food and a place to sleep. We all agreed that we would not stop until you were found."

She became quite sentimental. Trying to gain control, she spoke in a slurry speech.

"That makes me feel terrible. I was living in the richest conditions. Gladly, I would have given it all up for my family."

"Sweet Tal. Nobody blames you. There was nothing you could do. Nothing. Please don't fret over something you could not control. Do you understand?"

"Thanks, Twigs. I understand."

~

As the family ate supper, Oliver strolled in with the brightest disposition in years. Freya noticed immediately.

"What is it, dear? You actually look happy."

He grabbed his wife and put his face close to hers. "You're not going to believe this.

We received a substantial donation from an anonymous person. We are out of debt and well on our way to recovery and prosperity."

Freya's chair screeched to the floor as she jumped excitedly into his arms. She almost cried happy tears.

"That is not all. It seems the person who held Talia captive all these years wants to reimburse us for our dilemma. He sends his regrets and asks our forgiveness—and Talia's."

Talia's hand went to her mouth. She ran into Twiggly's arms and bawled her eyes out. He understood her tears and held her tight, rubbing her arms up and down.

"Dear child, I don't understand why you're so upset," Oliver told Talia. "Please tell me those are happy tears."

She stood up and wiped her tears. "Oh, Father. You probably won't understand. I realize that I was abducted, but the second time, my captor was really good to me. I knew he was suffering from a tormented past, and I had no choice but to consider that. I spotted a goodness in him, even though he tried to hide it. His house staff adored him and were very loyal, just like we are here. They were family, too. I grew fond of them, even though I missed you all something fierce. Seeing the human kindness that he never wanted anyone to see makes me happy. I just am blown away by how he is still, to this day, concerned about me and my family. As strange as this sounds, I wish I could see him and the staff again—just to thank him and tell them goodbye. The ultimate wish would be for all of us to get acquainted and keep in touch, but that, I daresay, would require fasting for a year."

"Tal, I don't like this talk. You sound as though you're fond of this monster who kept you from us all these years," Freya responded with a questionable look.

"He is not a monster, Mother! Don't you say such a thing."

"What in the world has gotten into you? He stole your teen years from you, and he stole you from us. Do you have any idea what we went through?" her mother replied, her voice rising.

"Yes. I'm sorry, and I understand how you must feel. At first, I hated his guts, arrogance, and general being. But as the years went on, he became caring and apologetic. Even still, he would never explain why I became his prisoner, but never once did he hurt me, except my pride. I almost got him to tell me why he chose me as his victim, but he realized quickly what he was about to say and stopped speaking.

"All I know is that around New Year's, he turns into some kind of a beast at the memories of this date. It's heartbreaking and gut-wrenching to watch, and nobody has been able to break through his built-up torment. I don't think I am to blame, but I'm sure I am connected to his anguish. That's all I can tell you."

Oliver clapped his hands. "That's enough. We certainly do not want to meet this monster—or for you to ever be in his presence again, Talia. Now, let's just drop this whole conversation." He turned to his wife. "Goodness, Freya. Can't you see what this talk is doing to her? As much as I detest the man, he *is* trying to make up for her abduction. Though the money can never repay us for our mental anguish, it seems that this is his way to correct his bad deeds. So, we should accept and move on with our lives. Now, I wish to speak of this no more."

Oliver turned and walked off. Freya scrunched up her mouth, then turned and walked off, too.

Talia and Twiggly looked at each other and shrugged their shoulders.

Chapter Thirty-Three

The following week, Freya, Adelaide, and Talia went shopping. Talia needed to stand out at the party tomorrow, so she planned on buying the perfect gown.

Later that night, Twiggly was given a bunce and took Adelaide out on a night in the city. They dined and danced. He escorted her to the River Coln, and they walked hand in hand. Eventually, Twiggly found a bench, and they sat down. Then, suddenly, he jumped down on his knee and held up a small, ornate box.

Her hand covering her mouth, she gasped.

"Adelaide, my true love, would you please be my bride?" His face was sweet, yearning, and bright with love.

She rubbed his face, choked up, and replied, "Yes, oh yes, I will."

They hugged and kissed. Then, hand in hand, they returned to the house and made an announcement. "Sir, before you leave for your business trip, we have some news." Twiggly's voice was loud, drawing everyone into the foyer.

"What is it, Twiggly? I am in a hurry," Oliver said curtly.

"Yes, sir. Adelaide and I are to be married."

"Good news indeed, old man." Oliver shook Twiggly's hand and pulled him in an embrace.

Freya and Talia joined them in a group hug. The thrill of the news just added to the excitement of the party at Chatwin's estate tomorrow.

Chapter Thirty-Four

C hatwin mingled with his guests. Hugs. Kisses on the cheek. Endless explanations.

Single women lined up to greet the Marquess—and married women, too.

Suddenly, all the guests became quiet. It was so silent, you could hear a pin drop. The guests faced the entrance to the party. Chatwin looked to see what was happening, and suddenly, he understood.

Like the other guests, he stared in her direction. Then, he walked slowly toward Talia with a bouquet of wildflowers. She looked like an angel from heaven. Her white gown glittered in a way that only added to her natural sparkle. The fabric was soft and matched her movement. The low back added some tease. Her hair hung down one side with a braid wrapped around her forehead that looked like a crown, with tiny, white flowers intertwined through it.

Chatwin inhaled deeply, feeling his heart pound like a drum. He patted the voice changer nestled in his tie to ensure it was still there. Though he was thrilled to see her, he didn't want her to identify him as 'good sir.'

Bertie and Poppy were not allowed to speak with or meet any guests in case their names made it back to Talia, but they peeked out from another room, spying on the party—thrilled to see Talia again.

Talia stood silent, waiting for Chatwin to greet her. Her heart was beating rapidly. She took a deep breath to steady herself. The last time they spoke, she was a child. *My, how handsome he is. Lord, protect my heart.*

When he reached her, he extended his hands and presented her with a bouquet of beautiful wildflowers. She accepted them, sniffed them, and smiled.

Finally, she mustered up the nerve to speak. "You look nothing like the boy I used to beat up as a child."

They both snickered.

"I must admit, you look nothing like that string-bean girl who annoyed me every day, and you most certainly did *not* beat me up. I allowed it to look like you won since I was raised to never hit a woman. I guess, girl, rather, would be more appropriate back then."

"Hmmf." She sighed. "I'm pretty sure you enjoyed our escapades as much as I did."

"That would be true. You are breathtaking, my lass."

Her soft pink cheeks glowed. "And you are beyond handsome, if I may add."

"Thank you kindly."

She held out the bouquet. "How did you know?"

"You mean all the times we had to stop and pick wildflowers as children? It was as routine as brushing my teeth." Her adorable giggle caused him to smile.

"Where have you been all this time?" she asked sincerely.

"Since my parents passed away, our beautiful town began failing. Then, I realized that getting us back on our feet was up to me. Luckily, I think I am succeeding. We should be making profits within the year, if not sooner."

"You didn't answer my question—about where you were, and why didn't you get in touch with my father while you were away —to explain that you would be back to help the town?"

"I was in a bad way when I lost my wife, and I couldn't deal with all the needs of this village at this time. I had to get away. I couldn't deal with my own situation."

"I can understand that. From what I understand, though, these citizens understood and supported you wholeheartedly, even while you were gone. I'm so sorry for what you went through."

"Thank you, but I can finally come to terms with my tragedy. When I got myself together, I realized I couldn't sit back and watch this town fall apart. It is my duty to protect these dear folks. But, on another note, how are you doing?"

"Couldn't be better, so thank you for asking."

"Were you subjected to filthy conditions and abusive treatment?" Chatwin asked.

"At first, I was, but this man rescued me and provided me with more than I could have asked for or wanted. He never told me his name and was always in disguise, but he cared for me. I wanted for nothing."

"And where is this mystery man now?"

She dropped her head for a moment before answering. "I have no idea whatsoever.

It appears he wants nothing to do with me. I suppose I was a thorn in his side."

"You? That could never happen."

She managed a half smile, but it faded quickly.

"Well, now that we're both back from the dead, perhaps we should make plans to spend time together as often as possible," Chatwin declared.

"Why?" Talia asked.

"Why should we spend time together?" He chuckled. "Since we are old friends, I thought we could rekindle our friendship."

"Oh, certainly. I would love to be your friend."

"You weren't thinking I was asking you out on a date, were you?"

Blushing, she replied, "No, no, that is silly. We don't even know each other anymore, but I would very much like to get to know you and be your friend again."

"Well, is there a man in your life?" Chatwin asked. *Please say no.*

"No, but there is a thought of one."

"Any chance you care to elaborate?"

"There is nothing to it. He doesn't even want me around."

"What makes you think that?"

"He told me he never wanted to see me again, and he has not come looking for me since we have been apart."

"Whoa! Surely, you are not talking about your abductor."

Talia just looked down at the floor.

"You were in a relationship with him?" Chatwin asked.

"No. Nothing like that, but...well, my heart will always belong to him."

"What a strange situation, and the ambiguity leaves a lot to the imagination. I must admit. I am curious about this mysterious abductor and your relationship with him."

"Like I said, we weren't in a relationship. I was an annoyance to him and nothing more. I do not wish to speak of this anymore, please," Talia said, looking up into his eyes.

"As you wish. Let's go mingle for a while." He extended his hand, and she accepted it.

~

During the evening, Chatwin couldn't take his eyes off her. Every male in the place flirted with her, and every female flirted with him.

Talia noticed him watching her from the corner of her eye, which made her uncomfortable and nervous. His features were striking, unlike the beast she fell in love with. *I could be myself with the good sir*, she thought. Now, amid all these people, she felt vulnerable, on display, and uncertain how to act.

Had she and Chatwin been away from each other too long? They were strangers. It felt awkward, and her heart was still saddened with grief from missing the good sir.

Still, the party was a huge success. As the night drew to a close, Chatwin approached Talia and said, "May I have a word with you in private, please?"

Talia nodded, and Chatwin escorted her into his office.

In his office, he motioned for her to sit on the luxurious leather sofa across from his desk. She sat, and he sat beside her.

"Talia, the party seems to be going well, but I couldn't help but notice that you look unhappy. I would assume that you'd be happy, escaping the circumstances you were in. May I ask what is bothering you?"

She almost cried, but she took a deep breath and suppressed her tears. "Truthfully, I don't know any of these people—not anymore. People change. I just don't feel I fit in here. And before you lecture me about giving it some time, I am very aware that it takes time to adapt."

"Well, you're wrong. I had no intention of lecturing you. In case you haven't noticed, I am sort of in the same boat. These people are like strangers to me, too. Even you—you're a stranger. I understand the awkwardness more than you think."

"Of course, you do," Talia said, touching his shoulder. "Forgive me. How insensitive that was for me to say. Maybe we should hang out and get to know these dear people again. I have an idea; what would you say to taking a boat ride with me tomorrow evening?"

"I would love to. Any destination in mind?"

"Yes, I'd like to take you to my fondest place in the world, but you can never tell or show anyone this area. You must promise me before I take you there."

"Cross my heart. Now you have given me something to look forward to. Until tomorrow evening, then."

She nodded her head, and he escorted her to the door.

Chapter Thirty-Five

The day after the party, Talia learned that her mother had made many plans for her. Talia's days and evenings would be booked solid in the coming weeks. Though she didn't want to disappoint her mother, her heart grew heavy because she didn't want to be the center of attention. She just wanted to get to know her friends and family again. Was that too much to ask for?

She wanted to tell her mother how she felt—that she believed her mother was more concerned about fitting in with the socialites than just being a mother. But to be fair, Talia had missed all her teen years, and her mother was trying to help her recapture some of it. Even though it wasn't the lifestyle Talia would choose, she decided to go along for her mother's sake.

At least she only had one engagement today—her boat ride with Chatwin.

On the way to her cherished spot, Chatwin pointed out a sign saying, "No Trespassing. Violators will be prosecuted."

"Oh no," Talia said, devastation evidence in her voice. "Someone is going to destroy my special spot." She just knew a fancy resort or development of some kind would take its place. "This is sacrilegious. As a child, I found a sign hidden by an overgrown brush named 'Cordina.' I always wondered what it meant."

Chatwin knew Cordina referred to his grandmother's family name since it was her property, but he would never divulge that information to Talia.

"Maybe the area will be preserved," he said, trying to comfort her, though he wasn't doing a very good job of it. The land now belonged to his family, which was his secret. She didn't know that he was building a stone cabin—actually, a castle just like the one he kept her prisoner in by the Irish Sea.

They had a lovely visit at Talia's spot, and Chatwin had vowed to keep her special place secret and untouched. And, of course, he hoped that she would marry him one day, though he had to get her to fall in love with him as Chatwin and not 'good sir.'

Back at her house, Chatwin saw the gerbil and rabbit. "Are these the same critters you had when we were children?"

"Crazy, right? I think it was the drops from the Dew of Heaven that have kept them so healthy."

"What are their names?"

She blushed. "Don't get a bigger head than you already have, but the rabbit is Prince Chatwin."

He already knew that information, but he formed a shocked face. "Why would you name him that?"

"As a *child*, I had a crush on you. Then you got too busy to hang out with me, so my parents bought me some critters. Since I missed you so much, I named one after you. The gerbil is Itsy."

"How terribly sweet."

"Terribly and sweet don't actually go together in a sentence."

He laughed at her mischievousness.

"Never mind. These are my mice," Talia said. "Come here, Tidbit," she called out in a sing-song voice.

Tidbit scurried over to Chatwin, who reached his finger through the cage and brushed his fur.

Talia's eyes grew big. "Just how did you do that? He never comes to anyone but me."

"Charm, what else?"

"Like you said, what else," Talia replied.

They laughed.

~

Chatwin saw Talia a few more times, but she seemed to be moving on with her life. Being that they lived in a small town, he knew she had been dating, which took a toll on his heart. From what he heard, she wasn't becoming serious with any of her suitors, but still, thinking of her spending time with other men hurt his heart.

Chatwin was thinking about Talia and the chasm of separation between them in his chambers one day when Bertie knocked on the door.

"Come in," Chatwin called.

Bertie opened the door, entered, and said, "Thank you, sir. I have paperwork for you to sign. The finishing touches should be done within a month. Any changes with the angel? Have you captured her heart?"

"She doesn't seem interested in me. Luckily, I don't think she's interested in her other suitors either, but I fear I may have lost her. I'm having a small get-together tomorrow evening where I plan on asking her if she could ever see herself having feelings for me. In my few conversations with her, I've discovered that she's stubbornly set on loving the good sir."

"Maybe you should tell her who you are. It's been a long enough time."

"I can't do that, Bertie. I just can't. Why can't she love me as Chatwin? I'm the same person she fell in love with at the castle. I didn't realize this was going to be so difficult."

"She doesn't know that you are *him*. Therefore, to her, you are another man, and unfortunately, she has no desire to open her heart to another man, Sir."

"I fear she was right when she told me that fairy tales *do* exist. She was referring to *Beauty and the Beast*. She actually loved the monster that I was then. If only we could go back..." His head dropped slightly.

"Not telling her the truth would be a mistake, your Lordship. Honesty is important to the girl."

"Bertie, have you looked at her? She is no girl. Besides, her heart could not take the truth right now."

"I will leave you to your thoughts, sir."

"Good day, Bertie."

~

Chatwin was fuming the next evening at the get-together, watching guys flirting with Talia. The turnout was bigger than he expected, as the guests he invited seemed to bring along others without his permission.

Already aggravated, his face scowled into anger when a handsome young man approached Talia. Chatwin watched Talia smile and laugh with the man, and when she placed her hand on his shoulder, Chatwin's breaths became labored with fury.

Chatwin plastered on a forced smile and approached Talia and the young man. "Excuse me. I hate to interrupt, but may I speak with you privately for a moment, Talia?" he asked.

She nodded her head and turned to the young lad. "It was great seeing you again, Drake. I look forward to our date."

Chatwin swallowed hard and escorted Talia into his study. After she sat down on his couch, he closed the door and turned to her. "Talia, would you be interested in going out with me? Like on a date—a real date... not just as friends?"

"Oh, that's so sweet, Chatwin, and yes, that may be fun, but it may be a while before we can find a time to get together. I've actually made plans every weekend with Drake for the next two weeks. He doesn't waste any time," she replied with a giddy smile.

"What's so great about Drake? You would rather spend time with him than me?" he asked forcefully.

"Don't go getting all tetchy with me, Buster. We're just friends. Would you rather spend time with your brother or a mouthwatering date? Surely you understand that?"

"You think of me as a brother?" His mouth dropped. *What did I do wrong?*

"Oh, Chatwin, you grouch." She stood, walked to him, and kissed his cheek. Then, she twisted strands of his hair playfully. Her eyes widened. "Why do you have a picture of a wolf in here?"

Feeling her touch, his stomach performed a somersault. "Ah... uh... oh, the wolf. That was actually my pet."

"You have a pet wolf?" Talia asked incredulously.

"Well, I did. The poor thing's mother was killed, so we cared for him. I named him Mr. Howls. When I got him, he was always standoffish, not willing to accept much affection. Then, one evening, as we slept, we heard screaming and growling. We all ran down the stairs to see Mr. Howls growling with his teeth exposed at two men, who were obviously there to rob us. The one man pulled out a gun, but Mr. Howls jumped on him and chomped on his arm."

"Oh, my goodness," Talia said.

"The shrilling yells of pain were frightening. Then, the other stupid man pulled out his gun, too, and Mr. Howls also disarmed him, but unfortunately, the gun went off, and Mr. Howls was killed."

"Oh, I'm so sorry," Talia replied. "What happened to the robbers?"

"Father confiscated their guns, and Mother called the Bobbies. Anyway, Mr. Howls saved our lives that night, so he was dear to my heart. I just wish I had the Dew of Heaven to give him back then. Maybe he would still be alive today."

"That is a sad and precious story."

"Yes," he said. "I supposed I should get back to my guests. Will you call me when you have some free time, and maybe we can spend some time together?"

"Sure," Talia replied.

Back in the courtyard, Talia immediately left Chatwin's side and returned to Drake. Once again, Chatwin stared in horror as she giggled with him.

Chatwin was still in the grips of fury when one of his staff members approached him and said, "Sir, we have run out of the crab appetizers but still have plenty of the shrimp."

Chatwin robotically replied, "Good to go."

"We'll have some more crab appetizers prepared in thirty minutes or so, sir."

"Yes. Yes," Chatwin replied absently. "We're good to go, then?"

Talia was walking toward the waiter with a tray of appetizers, and just as she met Chatwin, she heard his response to the kitchen worker. She froze. Drake, who was behind her, said, "Talia, Talia? Are you okay? Do you still want some shrimp?"

Talia stared at Chatwin. Apart from the good sir, she had never heard anyone say that phrase.

It couldn't be, she thought. *He couldn't be him. It's impossible.*

Staring into his eyes, she tried to imagine him with unruly hair, a beard, and a hoodie. She forced herself to look away from him, and she glanced around the room, spotting a portrait of Chatwin as a young teenager. His smiling parents stood beside him in the photo. Without saying a word, she marched toward the portrait and stood before it. His parents and the young teen's eyes looked more familiar to her now. She rubbed her jaw as she stared, trying to compare them to her memory.

Behind her, she heard Chatwin's voice, and she turned to see a gorgeous brunette woman speaking and laughing with him. *He really is attractive*, Talia thought. As soon as the thought popped into her mind, her heart filled with disappointment. *No. The good sir already has my heart.* Still, it bothered her to see the woman flirting with him—and he was obviously flirting back with her. *I've always had his undivided attention.*

As Talia stepped closer to hear their conversation, Chatwin kissed the woman's hand and stared into her eyes. "Until tomorrow," he said. "Good to go?"

She smiled back, giggled, and repeated, "Oh yes, good to go."

Talia was speechless.

"Talia, Talia. What are you doing? Are you listening to me?" Drake questioned her.

Continuing to stare at Chatwin, Talia ignored Drake, and he finally walked off, disgruntled by her obvious rejection.

Good to go? It couldn't be. He couldn't be... But he is. It has to be him, she thought through labored breaths. She braced her hand on the wall to steady herself, and then, she took a deep breath, donned a perfect smile, and devised a plan.

In her most tantalizing walk, Talia sauntered over to Chatwin. He smiled nonchalantly, and she said, "I've changed my mind."

"I'm sorry, you what?"

"I changed my mind. I *will* go out with you. How about tomorrow evening?"

"I...uh...I already have plans," he stuttered.

"How about the weekend then?"

"I...uh...I have plans then, too."

She put her hands on her hips and curved her lips into a pout. "A few moments ago, you had all the time in the world to be with me. How could that have changed so fast?"

He noticed the woman waving goodbye, and he looked at her, smiled, and nodded at her. Talia followed his gaze.

"Oh, so *she* is what changed your plans?" Talia demanded.

"Hold on before you misconstrue everything," Chatwin said, now focusing on Talia. "You told me you had plans with Drake. Since you clearly pointed out that I am nothing more than a brotherly acquaintance to you, I just figured my interests needed to go elsewhere. I'm really sorry for the confusion."

"Is that right? Look, I thought it over, and the expression on your face made me feel bad, so I decided it would be nice for us to spend time together."

"I'm sorry, Tal, but plans have been arranged. I can't break them."

A wave of jealousy shuddered through her body. *Now I know you're the beast,* she thought. *And now you're done with me? Just like that?* She smoothed her hair and feigned indifference. "No problem. That's probably for the best. Drake and I plan to have fun —*lots* of fun."

She turned around to walk off when he said, "Good to go, then?"

She bit her lip and refused to turn around and look at him. "Yes, good to go," she said, but as she stomped away, she thought, *You beast! He's saying 'good to go' right before my face. He's the only person I've ever heard say that, so he wants me to know it was him. I can't believe my childhood friend kidnapped me, beat me down mentally, and now has the nerve to show up without explaining any of it. How could he be so clueless and heartless?*

She approached Drake, kissed his cheek, put her arm in his, and snuggled up close. *If that doesn't bring out the beast in Chatwin, nothing will,* she thought.

Chatwin watched as she cozied up to Drake. Fury swept over him, and his face turned red. As he stomped up the stairs to his room, the house staff moved quickly out of his way with widened eyes.

Peeking through the door to the house staff quarters, Bertie saw the whole interaction. He turned to Poppy and said, "Oh, no. This is bad."

Chatwin slammed the door so loudly, it vibrated into the nearby rooms and down the stairs.

"Better call the fire brigade," Bertie said. "It looks like our Lordship's face is on fire."

"Dear, dear Bertie. They are not referred to as the fire brigade any longer. You need to bring your mind into the present. They are called the fire and rescue service."

"Some things should be left alone, dearest Poopy."

Poppy smirked and shook her head. "You are enchantingly old-fashioned, my dear. Now, what are we going to do about our Lordship?"

"I don't know. I just don't know," Bertie replied sadly.

Chapter Thirty-Six

D uring the next month, Whitney Stanford hung onto Chatwin's arm, attending all social gatherings with him. Likewise, Talia spent all her time with Drake. Talia and Chatwin often attended the same events, and when they saw each other, they would look away, seemingly unaffected.

As Chatwin entered the country club for a party, he scanned the crowd for Talia. When he spotted her, he saw that her friends had encircled her, looking at her hand. Drake smiled and stood on the outside of the circle.

To Chatwin, it appeared to be a gathering of an engagement announcement. His hands flew to his stomach, and his head felt like it was holding bricks. "I can't do this," he whispered, turning around and walking back out the door. Outside, he moved faster, eventually breaking out in a run to get to his car.

Talia had seen Chatwin enter out of the corner of her eye, though she dared not acknowledge him. Then, when she saw him leave the club, she wondered what was wrong. *It doesn't matter,* she scolded herself. *You shouldn't be concerned about him. He certainly hasn't been concerned with me.*

Though Talia loved the bracelet Drake gave her, she didn't

want to lead him on. She tried to compel herself to love him, but she realized that matters of the heart cannot be forced.

As Drake pulled up to Talia's house to bring her home, Talia said, "Drake, I love the bracelet. I really do, but I cannot accept it. The truth is, my heart belongs to someone else."

Drake smiled and took the bracelet from her tiny hand. "I suspected as much, Talia. I really wish it would have worked out, but I appreciate your honesty, and I only want the best for you."

Lying on her bed, Talia stared up at the ceiling, thinking. This wasn't going well at all. Her hopes of making Chatwin jealous seemed to send him right into the arms of another woman. *Now what?* She rolled over, covered her head with a pillow, and cried.

Suddenly, her sadness transformed into rage. Sitting up against the headboard, she scolded herself. "Stop acting like a child and confront him. It's not fair that he stole my teenage years and walked away without any explanation. Oh, no. I will go see him tomorrow. He will face a different beast, other than himself, that is. I made up every excuse in the world to protect him, but who's protecting me? My heart? He wasn't just a beast —he was a thief—one who stole my heart and then discarded it like it was no more than a bag of garbage. No. He needs to be held accountable. How am I to move forward until I know for certain how he feels about me? Whether I like the outcome or not, there is no choice, and I have to face the consequences of whatever the *good sir* wishes."

Tidbit stood by her in his cage. She bent down and spoke to him. "Oh, Tidbit, he *did* want to spend time with me, but I told him he was like a brother to me. I didn't know who he was at the time. I can't lose him again. Oh, Tidbit, what should I do?"

Sitting on a couch in his chambers, Chatwin weighed his options. *Maybe I'll kidnap her again. No, you fool. She would hate me even more. She already thinks I abandoned her.*

Without thinking, he threw a glass, which shattered, to the floor. *Geez. Now, my staff will think I'm turning into the beast again. Then again, with my current state of mind, it's only a matter of time before the beast returns. I need to get out of here. This isn't a life for me or those I love. I should have never come back.*

He gathered his things and planned to tell his regular house staff that he was going home—the home where he could be himself and not hurt anyone.

Chatwin walked down the steps with a small luggage bag, his briefcase, and his phone.

Bertie approached him. "I was unaware of any business trip you had planned, your Lordship."

"It's not business. I dropped a glass, and it broke in my room. Would you mind getting someone to clean it up?"

"Of course, my Lord."

Chatwin put his hand on Bertie's shoulder and momentarily looked into his eyes but lowered his head, unable to face Bertie's scrutiny. "Look, old chap, I just have to get away—by myself. There is only one place I can do that."

"Sir, no. You cannot go back there. It will torment you, and it is not safe. Report after report is devastating. The estate is nothing but a jerry-built and crashing into the sea. Part of the house has fallen. It is too dangerous, sir." His voice was elevated now.

Chatwin swiftly wiped away an escaped tear. "It's no use. I can't do it. I can't live like this and ruin everyone's lives. You all deserve to be happy. I have arranged it so this staff can move into the new estate and be well cared for. Business will go on as usual. This is no life for me or you. I love you, Bertie. Please give my love to the rest of the staff." Tears trickled down his face as he turned away and walked to the door.

"Sir, please," Bertie begged, calling after him. "You are my family. Do you have any idea what your leaving will do to me? To us? What about the girl?"

With his hand on the doorknob, Chatwin didn't turn around to reply. "She is engaged."

Bertie's eyes popped open wide. "Sir, you will die and crash into the sea with your estate. You can't possibly want to end your life that way."

Chatwin turned around slowly and looked back at Bertie with sad eyes. "Yes, Bertie, I can."

~

Poppy walked into the room whistling a happy tune. "Bertie, we will be moving to our new home in a week. Isn't it exciting?"

When Bertie didn't answer, she looked over at him. He was doubled over, one hand holding his forehead, and a muffled sound coming from his throat.

She placed a hand on his shoulder. "What is it, my sweet Bertie?"

His wrinkled forehead and red eyes looked up at her. "The good sir, my adopted son is returning to the house. He wants to die. It's different this time. He wants to crash into the sea with his estate. We can't stop him."

Suddenly, Poppy heard the swishing of helicopter blades. "Oh no. Is that him? He's already left?" Poppy fell beside Bertie and cried, "If he wants to die, that's the best place to do it. He'll never survive there. Oh, Bertie, I have never seen anyone tormented with such anguish as he."

"He said we deserved to be happy," Bertie said through tears. "It is not a selfish act. Poppy, he really believes this is for our wellbeing—an act of unselfishness to protect us from his angry rants."

Chapter Thirty-Seven

Back at the estate, Chatwin was shocked to see the destruction caused by his enemy, the sea. As he stepped out of the chopper, howling wind and waves crashed with such ferociousness it caused him to jump.

"Go ahead, take it all," he yelled. "Take me. You win. You're more of a beast than I. Live with that."

The sea grew wilder, and portions of the cliff crumbled into the water as Chatwin walked into the house. He surveyed each room, and his stomach turned, seeing the damage to Talia's tower.

"You coward! You devil! Sure, you wanted to take her away from me, the one thing that would hurt the most," he screamed. "You piece of vile vomit. Well, you can't have her! She's safe, so take that!"

He stomped up the stairs to his room.

Chapter Thirty-Eight

Talia jumped out of bed and showered quickly before losing her nerve. She threw on clothes and left the house without any brekkie.

She pushed the intercom button to the gate, and the gate opened slowly. She inched her moped closer and squeezed inside the gate, too impatient to wait for it to open fully. At the door, her shaking finger rang the doorbell over and over.

Finally, a butler came to the door. The butler stared for a minute. "How may I help you, Ms. Talia?"

"I need to speak with Chatwin, please, sir. It's urgent."

"I'm sorry, miss, but he has left the estate. I was informed he would send information later with our itinerary, but nothing of his. He left suddenly without warning or without any notice."

"So you have no idea when he'll return?" she asked, fidgeting.

"I'm sorry, but that is all the information I can provide you."

"Very well. Thank you for your time. Please tell Chatwin I need to speak with him immediately when you hear from him. I will check back tomorrow. Godspeed, sir."

She drove the moped back home disappointed. When she arrived home, the door felt like it was made of solid cement as she opened it.

"Where have you been, Tal? Don't take off without telling us first. We could never bear to go through something horrible again."

"I'm sorry, Mum. I went to visit Chatwin."

"This early in the morning? Surely, he isn't even awake."

"He's always busy with his affairs during the day, so I thought I would catch him before all that, but I was too late. He left town suddenly. I'm certain he left for business, but I don't know when he'll return. I suppose it really isn't any of my business where he went."

"Why would you need to know where he is, anyway? What's so urgent?"

"Hhhh," she sighed. "Mum, let's just forget the whole thing. Please."

Freya looked at her, trying to decipher her daughter's face. "As you wish, my dear. How about we get some breakfast?"

"I'm not hungry, so I think I'll go to my room."

"Tal, is there anything you would like to talk about?'

"No thanks. I didn't sleep well last night; that is all."

"All right, my dear. Get some rest."

Chapter Thirty-Nine

The next morning, Talia sped down the roadway on her moped. She was so deep in thought, she didn't notice the jogger and almost ran right into him. Her brakes squealed, and she stopped just in time. He let out a few expletives and raised a fist at her. "I'm so sorry," she yelled, but the jogger waved his hand downward forcefully and ran away. Then, she drove forward but had only traveled a few feet when she squealed the brakes again, almost running into another jogger. Face to face with the woman, Talia broke out into sobs. "I'm so sorry. I don't know what's wrong with me. Please forgive me."

"It's okay. You didn't hurt me. No damage done here."

"Oh, thank you, thank you. I'm sorry again."

"Are you okay, Miss?" the young lady asked.

"Yes. I'm fine. Thank you," Talia replied, and she drove off—very carefully this time.

At Chatwin's house, she paced back and forth before ringing the doorbell. "Courage, I need you." She reached for the buzzer, but the door opened before she could push it.

"Hello, Miss Talia," the butler said.

"Good morning to you."

"After the gate intercom buzzer went off, I was expecting

you. It seems I startled you, so I just want to clarify that for you."

"Ah, yes, now I understand why you were waiting at the door. Well, let's get right to the point so I don't keep you from much more meaningful tasks. Did Chatwin make it back yet?"

"I regret to inform you that he has not returned, and we have not heard from him. I'm sorry, miss, but I will be sure to give him your message when he does contact me."

"You don't think something bad happened to him, do you? Staff are always informed of his itinerary."

"No, Miss, I really don't, but I have not been with the good sir for very long, so getting to know his way of doing things will require some patience on my part."

"Well, thank you, sir, and I understand. Good day."

"Good day to you as well."

At home, on her way up the stairs to her room, she came face to face with Freya. "Not another sleepless night?" her mom asked.

"I'm afraid so, Mum."

"Talia, you must tell me what's going on. Does your mood have something to do with Chatwin?"

"No, Mum. I don't know how to explain my feelings, but please don't worry. I'll be my old self in a day or so. You have nothing to worry about. I only ask that you give me space to deal with my problems. I do not wish to speak with anyone—and I mean anyone, Mother. It will work out, and when it does, you'll be the first person I explain it to." She took her mum's hand, squeezed it, and then walked away.

In the kitchen, Freya said to her husband, "Oliver, maybe she'll talk with you. Something is really wrong. She should be out painting the town with her friends, going on dates. Heaven forbid any other gorgeous men should drop by and ask for a date. She declines all of them. Her friends called me and asked why Tal isn't answering their texts and calls. No social media in days. Now, that's a warning signal right there. What young person doesn't spend all their time on one of these, if not all?"

"Okay, my dear. I'll get up early and catch her before she leaves. Today and this evening, let's just let her be. Please don't worry. Our little lass has a very caring and good heart. She'll be just fine. You'll see."

~

The next morning, it was beginning to feel like Groundhog Day to Talia, reenacting the same day for the third day in a row. Except this morning, she wasn't expecting to see her father waiting for her, sitting on an entry chair covered in a paisley fabric and cushioned with an extra amount of goose feathers.

Talia jumped and put her hand to her chest. "Poppa, you gave me a fright."

"Forgive me, my dear daughter. I was hoping to catch you before you left. Now, I think we will have a talk before you leave. Please take a seat." He patted the cushion of the identical chair next to him.

The smell of bacon flowed through the house, and her stomach growled. She covered her stomach with a hand and sheepishly said, "Oops, didn't mean for my tummy to protest so loudly."

"It would appear your stomach is mad with you for not filling it lately."

She giggled.

"Now, I'm not here to lecture you, but you need to speak with someone, so please let me help."

"It's not that easy. To be honest, the truth will enrage you. I have done nothing wrong, so you can ease your mind, but my current state of mind has to do with the person who has been caring for me all these years—the man who saved me from being raped by my first abductors."

"You mean the man who abducted you the second time?"

"Father, if I tell you what is going on, then you have to promise me that you will not turn him in. I need you to swear on my life."

"What kind of father could ever do any such thing, Tal?" His eyes were tender.

"The kind of father who loves his daughter."

"We went through so much trying to find you. It's hard to forgive someone who took away our most precious possession."

Her hand touched his cheek, and her eyes were soft and tender. "I understand. I really do, but I know there must have been a reason for him taking me. I know that sounds crazy, but I must find the truth. Please, Poppa. Just trust me."

Seeing the tenderness in his daughter's eyes, Oliver remembered the moment he knew he had fallen in love with Freya. "You remind me so much of your mother," he said quietly. "My dear, follow your heart, even if love takes you to the stars in the heavens or down into the depths of the sea. Reach high, my darling daughter."

Talia's eyes sprung open wide, and she looked up. *I get your message, Lord. I will reach all the way to heaven to follow my heart. Thank you, Lord.*

Oliver interrupted her prayer. "I'm just worried about you, Talia. What if you find out why he abducted you...and the reason tears your heart in two? What if...the reasoning concerns a loved one and will change your feelings about that loved one?"

Talia squinted her eyes. "What are you not saying, Poppa? Do you know something? Even if you don't tell me what you know, I will find out because...because...well, because..."

"Because you're in love with him."

"How do you know that? What else do you know?"

"Dear, sweet Tal. A person would have to be an idiot not to see that you are in love. And I'm not sure what I know, but if what I suspect is true, there is a wicked secret that this person has kept from you, and it will turn your life upside down."

Talia burst into tears. "Oh, Poppa, it was Chatwin. He is the person who abducted me. I call him... I have called him a beast."

"So it *is* as I suspected."

"What? How long have you suspected this?"

"Truthfully, I just started putting it together this past month. Tal, this secret he has will eat you alive. I'm more worried about how it will affect you than knowing he was the abductor." He lowered his eyes.

"I have an awful feeling, Poppa. My churning stomach tells me you're right—that it will tear me apart, but it doesn't matter anymore. The truth has to come out. If you know the truth, then I would appreciate it if you would tell me." She grabbed his hands in hers with a desperate plea. "Please, Poppa, let this end now."

As he looked down at the floor, tears spilled onto his cheeks. Then he tilted his head up and looked into her eyes.

She held her breath. "I'm ready to hear it."

"It is me. I am the reason he abducted you. I was the person who crashed into his wife and killed her."

"Hhhh!" Talia gasped, clutching her chest with both hands. She jumped up and paced in circles. Her father stood and put his hand on her, but she backed away and rubbed her forehead.

"I'm going to tell your mother and turn myself in tomorrow," Oliver said, and he fell limp on the chair. "There isn't a day that goes by that I don't see Lily's face as I crashed into her. Not a day." He covered his mouth and mumbled, "I'm sorry, Tal. I really am."

"So Mum doesn't know?"

"No. She never knew."

"It's all making sense now. That's why you quit drinking, and that's why Chatwin doesn't drink. Oh, Poppa, I don't know what to do, but let me speak to him before you turn yourself in. Promise me?"

He shook his head, unable to speak.

She cupped his face in her hands and looked lovingly into his eyes. "Poppa, you have lived the same life as Chatwin all these years—a life of total anguish, and for that, I am sorry. What you did was horrible, but I will always love you, and it will all work out. You'll see. Now, I must go to him. He needs me, and I do love him so. Nobody knows where he has gone, but I think I know where he may be. It may be a day or two before I return, so don't be worried. He won't hurt me." She kissed her father's cheek and walked out the door.

Chapter Forty

S he drove the moped to the gate and pushed the button to the intercom. When the gate opened, she drove in and stopped in the drive.

"Bertie and Poppy have to be here unless they left with him, but the butler said nobody knew where he was going," she said, talking to herself. "They *have* to be here. I'll go to the servant's entrance, march through that house, and find them. And nobody better think twice about stopping me."

Without knocking, she opened the door to the servant's entrance and walked in. In the butler's kitchen, she saw Bertie and Poppy sitting at the table, silently drinking tea, with a look of dread.

"Just as I thought. I knew you two were hiding on me."

They jumped up and embraced her.

"Why didn't you tell me you were here? Don't you know how much I have missed you? Didn't you want to see me?"

"Dear child, more than you could imagine. Chatwin would not allow us to contact you until he told you the truth, but he needed to gain your trust first. Then, when he found out you were engaged, he took off..." Bertie fell to the chair and dropped his head, too emotional to speak further.

Talia looked at Poppy. "What is he talking about? I'm not engaged."

Bertie turned around in shock. "But the Lordship came home and told us."

"When was that?" Talia asked.

"He said he walked into the country club, and all your friends were looking at your ring, and that Drake fellow was watching you with a big smile."

She tilted her head back and covered her gasp. "No! No! He gave me a diamond bracelet, but I returned it and broke things off. I saw Chatwin leaving the country club, but I never put two and two together. Are you saying he left because he thought I was engaged?"

This time, Poppy dropped her head and began to cry. "Our Lordship is in love with you. You brought life back to him, and you are taking his life away from him now."

"What are you saying?!" She grabbed Poppy's arms and shook her out of her emotional state.

"He went back to his castle to die," Poppy wailed. "The sea is destroying the estate, and he wants to go down with the ship, so to speak. He forbids us to follow him."

Bertie interjected. "We don't know what to do, but we've all decided to go get him. I hope it's not too late."

"What are we waiting for? Let's go!"

Bertie touched Talia's cheek. "You are heaven-sent, dear lass. A real angel."

Chapter Forty-One

A caravan of cars followed the road to the estate. Everyone on Chatwin's staff came. Talia rode with Bertie and Poppy, constantly praying that Chatwin was okay.

The clouds rolled in fast, and lightning crackled in the sky. Thunder roared as if giants played a destructive game of bowling in the clouds.

Talia jumped. "Bertie, do you feel fear from the sea? It feels like it is alive and demanding us to turn back."

"You noticed that, too, huh? My lass, it has terrified us for years. At first, it seemed calm and peaceful, but after a year of being here, it felt as though we were at war with it. Who can defeat the sea? We have no choice but to surrender."

Poppy gasped and sat still like a statue looking out the window.

"What is it, Poppy?" Talia asked, placing her hand on her arm.

All she could do was point her index finger, which was trembling.

Everyone looked in the direction and could see the cliff on which their home stood. Most of the cliff had fallen into the sea, exposing that parts of the house had crumbled. Talia slapped her hand over her mouth and squeezed her eyes shut. "Chatwin, please be alive," she whispered under her breath.

Bertie and Poppy placed a hand on each of her knees.

The gate was wide open, something Chatwin would never allow. Talia twitched with chills. The castle was dark, with no lights on anywhere.

"Is the electric turned off?" Poppy asked.

"No, I paid the bill yesterday," Bertie said.

"Maybe Chatwin decided to come back to us. Maybe he's not here," Talia suggested hopefully.

"I fear not, Lass. His helicopter is here," Bertie added somberly as he glanced over at it.

They stepped outside of the car, and thunder exploded immediately. Lightning lit up the sky, and the crumbling sound of the castle falling apart scared Talia so much that she screamed.

"There, there, Lass. It will be all right. Let's get in there fast," Bertie said.

She was first in the door and ran around with one thing on her mind—Chatwin.

Everyone else looked at all the damage and trembled. They could hear the roaring sea and watched the waves splash against the windows.

"Where is he? Help me find him," Talia yelled.

"Talia, I think we should check his room," Bertie said.

"Me, oh my, my beautiful kitchen is destroyed," Talia heard Charles say.

Talia's shoes clicked up the stairs, and then there was complete silence as she stopped abruptly at the door to his room. She had so much fear, but there wasn't any time to waste. She opened the door to his room and slowly walked in. The damage to the room was unbelievable, but she couldn't decide if it was from Chatwin's temper or the castle falling apart.

Her eyes surveyed the room slowly, worried about what

they would see. She suddenly opened her mouth to scream, but nothing would come out. Just then, Bertie stumbled into her. *Oh, thank God you're here,* she thought, holding Bertie's hand for strength. Together, they moved forward slowly, and soon, they spotted Chatwin sitting on the floor with his head tilted up. His eyes were closed, and his back was against the wall.

"Oh, Bertie." Talia turned and embraced him. "I can't look. He's dead. There's no movement."

Just then, Poppy arrived, and Bertie grabbed Talia's shoulders, moving her into Poppy's embrace. "I must go to him. Stay here."

Bertie approached him slowly and placed a hand on Chatwin's shoulder. Suddenly, Chatwin jumped, and his eyes opened wide. "I told you not to come. Leave me at once. This place is close to dropping into the sea. No land separates the house from the sea now. Look for yourself."

Bertie looked out the window and was struck with fear. "Your Lordship, we're here to save you. Please come with us."

"He's alive! I must go to him," Talia whispered to Poppy.

Poppy held Talia back. "Wait, my child. Let Bertie talk to him."

A wave hit the window with herculean power, shattering it to pieces. Even Chatwin jumped.

"Chatwin, you are more than my Lordship; you're like my adopted son. If you won't leave, I will stay by your side."

"No, you won't! I demand you leave now," Chatwin yelled.

"I will not leave you. I love you like a son."

Chatwin lowered his head, and tears trickled down his face. "How can you love a beast?"

Bertie softly rubbed his hair. "You're no beast. Just a victim of cruelty."

Chatwin handed Bertie a crumpled photo. "You never knew, did you?"

Bertie took the photo, uncrumpled it, and then stared at the photo. In a fit of heaving sobs, he fell onto the bed, too distraught to speak.

Talia and Poppy looked at each other. "I thought Bertie knew everything," Talia whispered.

"I did, too. I can't imagine what horrible atrocity was revealed to him just now," Poppy replied.

"Let me go to him," Talia said. Poppy let her go, and Talia moved slowly toward Chatwin. Chatwin wanted to roar when he saw her, but her natural sparkle caught him off guard. She was light in the darkness.

"Get out of here before the sea takes you with it!" His words were forceful.

"I will not leave you. If the sea takes you, it must take me, too."

"What about your fiancé? I'm sure he is not pleased with you being here."

"I broke it off with Drake. I don't love him, and he never asked me to marry him. I'm so ashamed of myself, but I wanted to make you jealous. I couldn't stand seeing you and Whitney spending time together." Her lip quivered.

The wind whipped through the room as parts of the tower fell away into the sea. They had to yell to hear one another over the howling wind.

"I broke it off with her, too. But how long have you known it was me who kept you a prisoner?"

She cracked a smile. "You are the only person I have ever heard say, 'Good to go.' Also, the portrait of your family—I'd seen one just like it when you first took me. I once snuck into your room, looking for your coffin or other secrets."

His mouth dropped.

"I figured out too late. Chatwin, whether you love me or not, I love you."

An earsplitting crash shook the house, and everyone braced themselves.

Bertie interrupted their conversation, holding the photo.

"Sir, why didn't you tell me? Why did you hold onto this secret all by yourself?" His body rose up and down with sobs.

"I couldn't find the words. It hurt too much."

Talia looked at Chatwin and then Bertie. "Please, may I see the photo?" she asked.

Chatwin yelled, "No, you mustn't"—

But it was too late. Bertie handed her the photograph. Her hand covered her mouth, and a violent sob escaped her lips. Suddenly, she ran down the stairs out into the raging storm.

Chatwin jumped up and ran after her. "Talia, wait," he yelled.

Poppy walked over to the picture that Talia had dropped. She picked it up, stared at it momentarily, and cried softly. "No wonder he became a beast. He lost his wife and child all in one lousy second."

Poppy embraced Bertie, and they cried softly in each other's arms, but that didn't last long as a wave crashed through the window, soaking them.

"We need to get out of here now," Bertie said as he grabbed Poppy's hands and led her down the stairs to the outside steps.

Outside, everyone was waiting with questions on their faces.

"Did you see them?" Bertie asked.

"Aye. They ran that way. We tried to stop them, to no avail," Charles replied. "What's going on?"

Silently, Poppy passed the picture around.

Chatwin finally caught up with Talia, and he grabbed her fiercely, pulling her into him.

Into his chest, she blubbered, "You were never a beast. My poppa is the beast. I hate him for what he's done. I hate him!"

Lightning struck close by. Chatwin pushed away and tilted her face up to his. "No, you can't feel that way. Your father gave up everything for you—almost his life. He almost died from the anguish of losing you. Yes, I wanted him to feel the same pain I have lived with, but when you came into my life, I was able to heal and forgive. You're right. I do need you, and I do need my household staff... and I do need your God." His voice was gentle.

As he tried to force a smile, he held her chin and kissed her lips. She pushed back, sniffled, and looked down. "How can I ever look at you again after this? It's too painful."

"Because you understand God's forgiveness—and because I love you. I didn't think it was possible, but when you hold onto hatred, there is no choice but to feel anything but hate. Satan had a hold on me, but God sent you to me. I wanted to use you to ruin your father's life, and shamefully, I did, but now, my hate is gone. I won't press charges against your father, nor will I tell anyone about it. It's time to move forward. And you must, too."

"I can't. I can't," she said. "It's all too much."

"Talia, look at me. Look at me! You didn't know. You sacrificed your life, and you did it with grace and dignity. You may not be an actual angel, but among other people, you're as close as it gets. God loves you so much that He gave you this phenomenal presence to show you off. Not only does He love you, but so does every person you meet. And I love you."

Suddenly, they both felt the brush of an angel's wing softly caressing their bodies. They both stopped for a second and stared into each other's eyes with arched brows. When a wave splashed over them, the revelry was broken, and they shivered from the cold.

Chatwin wiped his face and asked, "Will you forgive me?"

"Will you forgive me and my poppa?" Talia asked.

"All done. All forgiven. And guess what?"

"What?" She managed to form a quick smile.

"I asked your God to forgive me. He is now my God, and I feel relieved and have a different outlook about everything."

"But you were willing to die."

"Yes, because I couldn't go through another loss. I thought you were going to marry Drake."

She rubbed his cheek tenderly. "I remember looking at you

through the window above the cliff, night after night. My mind played games on me because I really thought you were a beast at times—you know, like a real true *Beauty and the Beast*."

"Don't worry. I thought of myself the same way."

"It wasn't long before I realized I was in love with you, even at times when you terrified me so. Do you think you could really love me without feeling like you are betraying Lily?"

"Yes. She came to me in a dream and told me it was okay to be in love again. She wants me to be happy."

Talia nodded and smiled.

"I have a surprise for you. I must tell you about it. I can't wait anymore." Rain plummeted, lightning flashed, and the sea seemed angrier than usual, crashing violently over the land. "I have built a castle on the land you hold dear. It belonged to my grandparents, but our family inherited it, so it will always be our land. We will live there happily ever after, that is, if you'll marry me?"

He noticed the concern on her face.

"Don't worry. I built a stone fence around your sacred waterfall and what you call the *Dew of Heaven*. It looks like a secret garden, and nobody can ever destroy it. It's yours."

"No, it's ours," she said, grabbing his hand. "And yes. I'll marry you." She broke out into laughter.

"What's so funny?" Chatwin asked.

"I can't believe I am marrying the boy I used to beat up as a child—the boy who turned into the most gorgeous man I have ever seen and known."

"And I can't believe I am marrying the girl who drove me to annoyance—the most breathtaking woman in the world, inside and out. I am marrying the *Dew of Heaven* herself."

Chatwin held Talia's face and kissed her slowly, then more passionately. The feeling of lightning flashing through their bodies mimicked the lightning from the storm.

Just then, Bertie and Poppy approached them. Bertie pulled

them apart, hugged them tightly, and yelled, "I'm so happy for you. Now, get in the chopper right this instant!"

The caravan of cars sped away from the storm as Chatwin and Talia rose high above the rain in the chopper. The sea roared at them, but Chatwin smiled and yelled, "You lost. I have true love again!"

And they lived happily ever after at their beautiful estate, 'Dew of Heaven.'

$\sim$

Don't miss out on your next favorite book!
Join the Melange Books mailing list at
www.melange-books.com/mail.html

THANK YOU FOR READING

~

Did you enjoy this book?

We invite you to leave a review at your favorite book site, such as Goodreads, Amazon, Barnes & Noble, etc.

DID YOU KNOW THAT LEAVING A REVIEW...

- Helps other readers find books they may enjoy.
- Gives you a chance to let your voice be heard.
- Gives authors recognition for their hard work.
- Doesn't have to be long. A sentence or two about why you liked the book will do.

About the Author

Linda Phillips moved back to a winter wonderland in Wisconsin until a sneaky sunray snuck through the overcast clouds and beamed down on her, pulling her right back to sunny Florida. When she's not daydreaming about a sweet romance story, she tends to Monster I and Monster II, affectionately known as Sprinkle Dinkle and Skittle Wittle, her two cats.

lindalouphillips.com

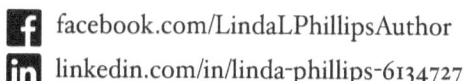

facebook.com/LindaLPhillipsAuthor

linkedin.com/in/linda-phillips-61347270

Also by Linda Phillips

WITH SATIN ROMANCE

Novels

Marry Christmas

Follow Your Heart

(A Stand Alone Fantasy Romance Series)

Moon Water

Dew of Heaven